A GHOST OF A CHANCE

MORGANA BEST

BEST
Cosy Books

A Ghost of a Chance
Witch Woods Funeral Home, Book 1
Second Edition
Copyright © 2020 by Morgana Best

First Edition Copyright © 2015 by Morgana Best
All Rights Reserved

ISBN 978-1-925674-04-0

manufacturer, or otherwise, specific brand-name products and / or trade names of products.

By this act
And words of rhyme
Trouble not
These books of mine
With these words I now thee render
Candle burn and bad return
3 times stronger to its sender.
(Ancient Celtic)

GLOSSARY

S ome Australian spellings and expressions are entirely different from US spellings and expressions. Below are just a few examples. It would take an entire book to list all the differences.

The author has used Australian spelling in this series. Here are a few examples: *Mum* instead of the US spelling *Mom*, *neighbour* instead of the US spelling *neighbor*, *realise* instead of the US spelling *realize*. It is *Ms*, *Mr* and *Mrs* in Australia, not *Ms.*, *Mr.* and *Mrs.*; *defence* not *defense*; *judgement* not *judgment*; *cosy* and not *cozy*; *1930s* not *1930's*; *offence* not *offense*; *centre* not *center*; *towards* not *toward*; *jewellery* not *jewelry*; *favour* not *favor*; *mould* not *mold*; *two storey house* not *two story house*; *practise* (verb) not *practice* (verb); *odour* not *odor*; *smelt* not *smelled*; *travelling* not *traveling*; *liquorice* not *licorice*; *cheque* not *check*; *leant* not *leaned*; *have concussion* not *have a concussion*; *anti clockwise* not *counterclockwise*; *go to hospital* not *go to the hospital*; *sceptic* not *skeptic*; *aluminium* not *aluminum*; *learnt* not *learned*. We have *fancy dress* parties not *costume* parties. We don't say *gotten*. We say *car crash* (or *accident*) not *car wreck*. We say *a herb* not *an herb* as we pronounce the 'h.'

The above are just a few examples.

It's not just different words; Aussies sometimes use different expressions in sentence structure. We might *eat a curry* not *eat curry*. We might say *in the main street* not *on the main street*. Someone might be *going well* instead of *doing well*. We might say *without drawing breath* not *without drawing a breath*.

These are just some of the differences.

Please note that these are not mistakes or typos, but correct, normal Aussie spelling, terms, and syntax.

AUSTRALIAN SLANG AND TERMS

Benchtops - counter tops (kitchen)
Big Smoke - a city

Blighter - infuriating or good-for-nothing person

Blimey! - an expression of surprise

Bloke - a man (usually used in nice sense, "a good bloke")

Blue (noun) - an argument ("to have a blue")

Bluestone - copper sulphate (copper sulfate in US spelling)

Bluo - a blue laundry additive, an optical brightener

Boot (car) - trunk (car)

Bonnet (car) - hood (car)

Bore - a drilled water well

Budgie smugglers (variant: budgy smugglers) - named after the Aussie native bird, the budgerigar. A slang term for brief and tight-fitting men's swimwear

Bugger! - as an expression of surprise, not a swear word

Bugger - as in "the poor bugger" - refers to an unfortunate person (not a swear word)

Bunging it on - faking something, pretending

Bush telegraph - the grapevine, the way news spreads by word of mouth in the country

Car park - parking lot

Cark it - die

Chooks - chickens

Come good - turn out okay

Copper, cop - police officer

Coot - silly or annoying person

Cream bun - a sweet bread roll with copious amounts of cream, plus jam (= jelly in US) in the centre

Crook - 1. "Go crook (on someone)" - to berate them. 2. (someone is) crook - (someone is) ill. 3. Crook (noun) - a criminal

Demister (in car) - defroster

Drongo - an idiot

Dunny - an outhouse, a toilet, often ramshackle

Fair crack of the whip - a request to be fair, reasonable, just

Flannelette (fabric) - cotton, wool, or synthetic fabric, one side of which has a soft finish.

Flat out like a lizard drinking water - very busy

Galah - an idiot

Garbage - trash

G'day - Hello

Give a lift (to someone) - give a ride (to someone)

Goosebumps - goose pimples -

Gumboots - rubber boots, wellingtons

Knickers - women's underwear

Laundry (referring to the room) - laundry room

Lamingtons - iconic Aussie cakes, square, sponge, chocolate-dipped, and coated with desiccated coconut. Some have a layer of cream and strawberry jam (= jelly in US) between the two halves.

Lift - elevator

Like a stunned mullet - very surprised

Mad as a cut snake - either insane or very angry

Mallee bull (as fit as, as mad as) - angry and/or fit, robust, super strong.

Miles - while Australians have kilometres these days, it is common to use expressions such as, "The road stretched for miles," "It was miles away."

Moleskins - woven heavy cotton fabric with suede-like finish, commonly used as working wear, or as town clothes

Mow (grass / lawn) - cut (grass / lawn)

Neenish tarts - Aussie tart. Pastry base. Filling is based on sweetened condensed milk mixture or mock cream. Some have layer of raspberry jam (jam = jelly in US). Topping is in two equal halves: icing (= frosting in US), usually chocolate on one side, and either lemon or pink or the other.

Pub - The pub at the south of a small town is often referred to as the 'bottom pub' and the pub at the north end of town, the 'top pub.' The size of a small town is often judged by the number of pubs - i.e. "It's a three pub town."

Red cattle dog - (variant: blue cattle dog usually known as a 'blue dog') - referring to the breed of Australian Cattle Dog. However, a 'red dog' is usually a red kelpie (another breed of dog)

Shoot through - leave

Shout (a drink) - to buy a drink for someone

Skull (a drink) - drink a whole drink without stopping

Stone the crows! - an expression of surprise

Takeaway (food) - Take Out (food)

Toilet - also refers to the room if it is separate from the bathroom

Torch - flashlight

Tuck in (to food) - to eat food hungrily

Ute /Utility - pickup truck

Vegemite - Australian food spread, thick, dark brown

Wardrobe - closet

Windscreen - windshield

Indigenous References

Bush tucker - food that occurs in the Australian bush

Koori - the original inhabitants/traditional custodians of the land of Australia in the part of NSW in which this book is set. *Murri* are the people just to the north. White European culture often uses the term, *Aboriginal people*.

he wages of sin is death!'

I jumped when I heard the blaring ringtone of my mother's mobile phone. Sure, we were outside a chapel, so it was an appropriate setting for such words, I supposed, but it was my father's funeral.

The service had just ended, and my mother was busy complaining to her captive audience about the minister's words. "This was a good opportunity for Pastor Green to witness to the unsaved," she said for the umpteenth time. "He spoke about nothing else but my husband, Larry, yet he calls himself an evangelist!"

I sighed and turned back to accept the condolences of people I had never met. I'd left home for college and had done my best not to return home from Melbourne since. Witch Woods was a small town in New South Wales, a two to three day drive from Melbourne. I'd grown accustomed to the hustle and bustle of city life, and that was one of the reasons I'd planned to stay in town for only a week or two, max. The main reason was my mother. For the sake of my sanity, I could not live with her day in, day out, for too long.

It also didn't help that I was able to see and speak to ghosts. A funeral home was not a good place for a person with such abilities, for obvious reasons. You would think a major city like Melbourne would be full of ghosts, and you would be right, but I was good at not letting on that I could see them. Ghosts always leave you alone if they think you can't see them.

However, in Witch Woods, the people, living and dead, knew me, so it was hard to pretend. The one saving grace was that most people crossed over to the other side as soon as they died, and it was only the ones with unfinished business who remained on this earthly plane.

My childhood had not been easy. My mother had been horrified that I spoke to my imaginary friends, which is what she called them, although she knew the truth. The ability to see ghosts happened to the daughters of every second generation in Mum's family. My grandmother had told me this when I was around ten years of age, just before she died. However, my own mother was in denial. She had taken me to child psychologists and even had me on medication for a while, until my father had put a stop to it. I had soon learnt not to speak to ghosts in front of anyone.

My mother's voice snapped me back to the present. "All we like sheep have gone astray," my mother said to a Goth teenager, who was backed up against a wall with no visible means of escape. "I'm not upset about my husband, as he's in a better place. But do you know where *you* will spend eternity?"

"Err, no," the teenager said, looking around frantically.

"Mum, Pastor Green wants to speak to you," I lied. The teenager shot me a grateful look and hurried away. I wouldn't fare so well. I knew I would pay for that later.

I was developing a nasty headache, and the noise level didn't help. There were so many people, I suppose because everyone knew Dad as he had the funeral home, and everyone from Mum's church appeared to be here as well.

Mum appeared at my side. "Liars and perjurers do not inherit the kingdom of God," she said loudly, pointing to me, and everyone turned to look.

My face burnt hot with embarrassment. I beat a hasty retreat and headed for the door that led to the kitchen, intending to refill the coffee pot. We generally served coffee, tea, cold drinks, and snacks to attendees after a funeral. Just as my hand closed around the doorknob, someone cleared their throat loudly behind me.

I swung around to see an elderly man, a cranky expression on his face. His clothes were old fashioned, like from fifties movies. His trousers were somewhat baggy, and he looked unkempt. He was wearing a frown. "Who are you?" he barked at me.

"I'm Laurel Bay," I said, extending my hand to shake his.

He backed away and looked at my hand. "Bay?" he repeated. "Are you Larry's daughter?"

I nodded. "Yes."

The man stepped forward and narrowed his eyes. "I haven't seen you around before."

Here we go again. I'd have to go through my life story one more time that day. "No, I went to

Monash University in Melbourne and stayed in Melbourne. I'm only back for Dad's funeral. And you are?"

"Ernie Forsyth."

I nodded. "Nice to meet you. Well, if you'll excuse me, I'd better get back to work."

Before I had a chance to leave, Ernie snorted rudely. "Work! Do you call this work? Does anyone around here actually know how to run a funeral home properly? Do you have any idea what your mother does with the profits? I'll have you know that I used to run a very successful funeral home, until I retired to Witch Woods. I gave your father my advice many a time, but he just wouldn't hear what I had to say."

I rubbed my temples. I didn't need this right now. "Well, thank you, Mr Forsyth, but—"

He cut me off. "You can call me Ernie."

"Okay, Ernie." I looked past Ernie to see two elderly ladies staring at me.

"Are you okay, dear?" the taller one said as she walked over to me, straight through Ernie.

*a*s I stepped into the lawyer's office, I was surprised to see how cramped it was. There was a desk near the back of the room, almost touching both walls, and two chairs sat in front of it. Just next to the door was a large bookcase that was leaning to one side, as though it might fall over at any moment. It had piles of important looking books on it, the kind you would certainly expect a lawyer to have.

The lawyer himself, Mr Goddard, was sitting behind his desk. He removed his reading glasses when I entered the room, followed by my mother. He squeezed himself between one end of the desk and the wall and made his way to us, extending his hand. After I shook his hand, I stepped aside for my mother to do the same.

"Please, have a seat, and we can get this underway. I know now is a time of pain and sadness, and I doubt either of you want to spend more time in here than necessary," Mr Goddard said. He was a large man with an immaculate goatee perched on his chin. His eyes were narrow and pale blue, and his brown hair thinning.

It was obvious to me that the lawyer was right about me not wanting to spend more time in his office than necessary. The place was so small that it felt like an elevator, and the whole room was stuffy. There was a window in the office, right behind the desk, but it was firmly shut. I spent a moment wondering if it would be rude for me to ask him to open it. I decided to suffer in silence.

My mother chose one chair, and I dropped into the other. I looked over at her, and saw her hand dip into her purse. She pulled out a white handkerchief, and dabbed at her eyes, a move I had seen plenty of times in the short time I had been home. It looked exactly like what a good grieving woman would do.

That wasn't to say I thought my mother wasn't

grieving, of course. I knew that she was. Whatever her faults, and there were really too many to list, she had loved my father, and he had loved her, for some reason I had never figured out.

"Thank you for seeing us a little earlier than you had planned," my mother said, smiling at the lawyer. "I have a church group function today, and I couldn't miss it."

Mr Goddard nodded as he sat back down at his desk. He folded his beefy hands on the desktop in front of him. "Church is important," he said.

"It is the most important thing I know of," my mother said, "but we don't see you there every Sunday, Henry. Shall we see you there this week?"

It was all I could do not to scream and dive through the window. I didn't have a problem with church in general; it was more a problem with my mother. Living through my childhood had been bad enough, being forced to attend the countless hours of church functions most days of the week. But to be back, and to see that my mother wasn't any different now than she had been when I was a child, creeped me out a bit, to be honest. It was fine to be religious, but she was a fanatic and not even a borderline one. If God were a business, she would certainly be the number one salesperson in the office.

The lawyer had a manilla folder on his desk. He flipped open the cover and pulled out a document that consisted of a good number of pages. I sincerely hoped he didn't intend to read each and every page. He picked up his reading glasses and set them on the end of his nose once more.

"Now your husband, and your father, of course," he said, nodding to each of us in turn, "has left a few things to others, and they will be notified in due course, but I thought we could go ahead and go through it since you two will be receiving the bulk of his estate, such as it is."

My mother and I both nodded, waiting for the man to go on.

"Thelma, you are to receive the residence behind the funeral home, the considerable sum of your husband's savings…" and the lawyer continued, while my attention drifted. Of course, my mother was to receive most of my father's things, if not everything. I figured he would leave me something, maybe his prized Gary Ablett Senior signed AFL football jersey. Football was something I only marginally cared about, but my mother didn't care at all, so my father had gravitated to me as his football buddy.

Indeed when the lawyer was finished with my mother and looked at me, the jersey was the first thing he mentioned. The second thing, however, took me by surprise.

"And also, Ms Bay, your father has instructed that you are to take over the day-to-day running of the funeral home. More precisely, he has left the funeral home, the acreage on which it stands, and the business, to you."

My mouth dropped open, and beside me my mother said, "What?"

I looked at her. She was as shocked as I was.

Mr Goddard went on. "Thelma, as I said, you are to receive the residence on the allotment behind the funeral home, but your daughter is being given the business itself."

"I can't run a business," I said.

"You're right!" my mother screeched. "You don't know the first thing about it. I've been by your father's side for years. And this is how he repays me? I'm so hurt. I'm so hurt that I'm completely speechless. How could he do this to me? He could never make a decision for himself. He didn't even discuss the will with me. In fact, I'm not sure this is even legal. I should be the one to take over the business."

"You can do it!" I said. "Believe me, I'll give it to you."

"Actually, hold up a moment!" Mr Goddard said as he raised a thick finger in the air, commanding our attention. We both looked at him, and he went on. "The deceased states that if Ms Bay is able but unwilling to run the funeral home, it will simply be put up for sale. She is the only person in the family he wanted to run it."

I looked at my mother. "Okay, we can sell it."

"Absolutely not!" my mother said. "With God as my witness, and of course, being the great Christian that I am, he is always my witness, but as God as my witness, no one but our family will ever run that business." She fixed me with a withering glare. "Laurel, I feel in my spirit that God is telling me to oversee the business and do periodic checks on you, to make sure you are indeed running it. I believe God is telling me that I alone should manage the purse strings."

"We can sell it," I repeated. "I don't even want any of the money."

My mother pulled another white handkerchief

from her purse and dabbed at her forehead. "No! What would I do after that money was gone? I need to work. I need that business."

"But if I run the funeral home, you wouldn't get money from it, anyway," I said, confused.

"If you ran it, obviously you would hire me as the general manager," my mother said sharply.

To be honest, I hadn't even considered hiring my mother. Not that I had ever thought about running the funeral home, but if I had, she's not someone I would hire. And I wasn't even sure the funeral home had ever had a general manager. That sounded more like a job you would get in retail. Dad had always done the lion's share of the work himself.

Behind his desk, Mr Goddard looked a bit uncomfortable. "That's all the will says," he said, rising from his chair, no doubt trying to get us to leave. I took the hint and stood, and my mother did the same. I shook the lawyer's hand and then my mother did, too.

My mother then leant over the desk, and peered into the man's eyes. "You know, I've been meaning to say this for a while. I suggest you look into changing your name. The name 'Goddard' is blasphemous. If you don't change it, I wouldn't expect you to be welcomed into heaven. I told Pastor Green of my concerns last year, and I'm surprised he didn't mention it to you."

The lawyer's mouth dropped open, but he quickly shut it. "I'll, uh, keep that in mind."

My mother nodded and patted his cheek. Then she turned and walked out of the office. I threw an apologetic look at the lawyer and followed her.

We had driven to the lawyer's office together, something I was now regretting. We climbed into my car.

"So, you can leave it all to me, but you can appear as though you're running the business just as a front," my mother said firmly, as I pulled into the street. "That was obviously what your father really wanted."

"What if the lawyer finds out?" I asked.

"Now, you don't need to be a little brat," she said. "You've caused me enough problems as it is. You took three days to be born, and you've given me trouble ever since. Did you know, a woman came up to me in the hospital bathroom and asked me if I'd had a boy or a girl? I was forced to admit that I hadn't had the baby yet. Do you have any idea how embarrassed I was? I knew then what I was in for with you. You caused me trouble then, and you're causing me trouble now." She paused and took a deep breath. "Well, we can make it look as though you're running it, but I'll do it."

I sighed. Mum always pulled out the three-days-to-be-born story when she was super mad with me. "Mum, I don't live here. I don't want to live here. I don't even live in this state. I have a life! I have another job."

She snorted rudely. "A retail store assistant? Hmpf!"

"Mum, you know I'm a jewellery valuer."

She pursed her lips. "Well, I won't sell it."

I shook my head. I got on the small two-lane highway and headed back to the small town in which I had grown up. Everything around here was small. It drove me nuts.

"It's not up to you, Mum," I said, quite bravely. "It's up to me, and I don't know the first thing about running a funeral home. Dad did it all. He embalmed until Janet came along; he hosted the gatherings. Everything. What am I supposed to do?"

"You need to do it, because I guess it's all up to you. But you cannot sell it."

"I'm going to sell it," I said quietly. "I can't see any other option."

"You need to pray more," my mother said in a huff. "Come to the church outreach meeting with me today."

"No," I said with enough severity that my mother let it go, and we drove on in icy stillness. When we got home, she got out in stony silence and went directly to her car. She pulled out of the drive and headed towards her church.

I went inside. The place was empty. No one was working that day. The business was dead, so to speak, while everything got ironed out. I walked down a long hall and then opened a plain white door. It led to a corridor, and I found myself in the embalming room. There was a slanted metal table there, and numerous tools that were foreign to me. Dad had spent a lot of time here. He prided himself on making people look as natural as possible after death, and he was very good at his job. Of course, as the business had grown, he had employed Janet to do that.

Dad wasn't around. He wasn't a ghost and I knew he wouldn't be one. The only people who stuck around were those who had been wronged or needed closure. My dad wasn't that kind of man, and as much as I would have loved to see him now and speak with him, I was glad he had gone on.

Yet standing in that cold room, it was almost as if he were still here. "I don't understand, Dad," I said aloud. "I don't know the business. I grew up in it, but I don't know it. I don't live here anymore. I don't want to. I don't want to live near Mum, or with her."

I shuddered at that thought. My words echoed off the plain walls and the table, and there was no answer to anything I was saying. I knew there wouldn't be, but it felt good to get it off my chest. I turned and headed back outside.

The expansive building that comprised the funeral home was tastefully furnished, designed to be open and to hold a lot of mourners. Out the back was our family home, and I made my way out there. I pulled a salad out of the fridge and sat at the small kitchen table. I felt more lonely than I had in a long time. I almost wished that the old man, Ernie, would come by, so that I'd have someone to talk to. I knew that wasn't how it worked, though. I was always on the ghosts' schedules, and they were never on mine.

I knew my mother was right. She had a nice sum of money now, but she couldn't live off it forever. If I sold the place, could we get enough for her to be set for the rest of her life? I had no idea.

As I sat there over an empty plate, nibbling on a tomato, I somehow knew I was going to stay. It dawned on me slowly, but I knew it to be true. I was going to stay, and as much as the thought upset me, somehow, a small part of me was excited.

CHAPTER 3

*T*he morning of my first memorial service as the owner of the funeral home started just like any other day, but something in my stomach warned me that this wouldn't last long. It was an awkward, funny sensation that kept bothering me, but I attributed it to the same nerves that I felt every time we held a service. I had never wanted to be part of the funeral business, and I wasn't enjoying being part of it now. I forced myself to ignore the feeling, and finished the last of the paperwork. I then headed out to the chapel floor.

I stood off to the side, watching the guests as they entered and took their seats. There weren't many people in attendance, but at least there were enough to fill most of the rows. As they filed in, another feeling came over me. It was almost like I was forgetting something, or someone.

With so much commotion going on around me that morning, I hadn't immediately noticed that the pastor wasn't yet at his podium to greet the guests. They were almost all seated, so I knew that I had to begin a frantic search to find him. As I skimmed every corner and crevice of the chapel, I noticed a slight ripple coursing through the large velvet funeral curtain.

I headed over to see what was going on, but when I slipped through the opening in the curtains and walked into the small area, I recognised the problem at once. Standing by the closed coffin were Pastor Green and a young man who was dressed in a tight-fitting, dark suit. He seemed to be holding back a stream of tears, and his voice was agitated.

"Please, Pastor, just for a minute or two?" he asked, fidgeting.

"I'm sorry, son, but this is supposed to be a closed casket funeral," Pastor Green said, shaking his head firmly. "The body was displayed for viewing all day yesterday. Once the casket is closed, I cannot allow it to be reopened without permission."

"I understand, Pastor Green, but I really just

want to say goodbye one last time before I go out there and face everyone," the young man said, rubbing his eyes hard. "It'll make reading this eulogy much easier," he added, holding up a small, worn sheet of paper.

By that point, I'd heard enough, so I walked over to them and cleared my throat. "Excuse me, Pastor Green," I said, hoping the kindly man wouldn't be upset by my intrusion. "I overheard your conversation, and even though it's against our policy to allow the casket to be opened after viewing hours, I'll allow it this time."

The look on the grandson's face went from one of devastation to that of relief and something else that I couldn't quite put my finger on. His tears didn't dry up completely, but he sure seemed to be in higher spirits. "Thanks so much," he said, his voice now less shaky. "Thank you."

"I'll go with you if you'd like."

He smiled and gently grasped my hand. As we approached the casket together, Pastor Green shot me a worried look from his position behind the coffin, but it wasn't that big of a deal, in my opinion. The grieving man only wanted to see his grandmother one last time. I couldn't blame him for wanting such closure.

I looked at the pastor and nodded, signalling for him to raise the lid. As it slowly lifted, I tried to keep my eyes towards the floor. I wanted to be there for moral support, but staring at the body was something that I could do without. I had seen enough death over the years to last me a lifetime, and I was sure I would see plenty more in the months to come. Moving away as I had, had only delayed the inevitable. It didn't stop this aura of death from surrounding me once more.

As my thoughts stayed focused on such things, I didn't initially realise what was going on all around me, but then everything seemed to happen in slow motion. At first, I only felt the grandson's hand release mine, but then I heard the screams as they quickly grew from quiet shrieks to deafening roars in no time at all. When the world around me finally came back into focus, I spun around, still uncertain what was happening. Pastor Green had a blank look on his face as he scratched his forehead.

"There's a body in the coffin!" the man screamed again, stumbling backwards towards the curtain as his hands flailed through the air. He took a few short breaths in quick succession before he hunched over with his hands on his knees.

"Of course there's a body in there," Pastor

Green said in a calming tone. "It's your dear grandmother. She's departed this life, and that's why she's in the casket." His attempt to soothe the man did not work at all.

The grandson lifted his hands as he sprang back up, covering his face. With his sight obstructed, he turned around too quickly and tripped, sending his body once more towards the curtain.

I watched everything unfold right before my eyes, but I lacked any real power to stop it. He fell into the curtain, entangling himself even more as he struggled to get free. Seconds later, the curtain flew open, revealing the startling scene to the entire chapel of guests. It was then that I noticed what he was reacting to at the very same time that everyone else did.

There was a body in the coffin all right, but not only the one that was supposed to be in there. The second body came with a large knife jutting from its back.

The sound of gasps quickly expelled all chatter from the room and then a dead silence engulfed the room. I turned around to see the shocked faces of every guest as well as staff member of the funeral home. They all stood in fright as the silence turned to sobs and gasps. The only person who didn't look completely horrified was Pastor Green.

The poor man looked at me intently and threw his hands up in a display of confusion. "I think the boy is clearly stressed and that's caused mass hysteria."

Indeed, the young man was stressed, but for good reason. Pastor Green was standing behind the tall lid of the coffin as it stood raised, obstructing his view from the horror that everyone else in the room could see. I quickly extended a hand to the grandson, but Mum appeared out of nowhere before I even had a chance to assist him.

"Help me with this curtain!" she snapped, staring at me with fire in her eyes. I stood up, pulling the man to his feet as I did. I rushed over to the right side of the curtain and helped her pull it closed to conceal the coffin once more. "Pastor Green, did you not see the girl in the coffin that was right under your nose? I knew I should have overseen this service," she added, her gaze making sure I knew that the comment was directed at me.

Pastor Green looked frustrated. "Thelma, let's just get everyone calm and figure out what happened."

Mum turned and glared at me again, wagging

her finger inches from my face this time. "You just came back into town and your very first funeral turns out to be a nightmare like this?" she said. Her voice was laden with suppressed anger.

"Oh my," another voice said, chiming in. I looked over to see Janet, the funeral home's cosmetician, her mouth agape as she pushed through the curtain and approached the casket. "That looks like the girl from the café in town. I wondered why I found a tray of cold coffee by the door this morning."

"That might very well be the case," Mum said, "but that's hardly of any importance right now. Would you please call the police and let them know what happened here?"

"Sure." Janet pulled her mobile phone from her pocket as she headed towards one of the back rooms for privacy.

"And Pastor Green, please close that casket already so more people aren't horrified by that corpse. And why was it even opened in the first place? Isn't this supposed to be a closed-casket event? Wasn't the viewing yesterday?"

I stepped towards my mother with my hand raised in an attempt to quiet her so I could speak. "Yes, it was, and the coffin has been closed since,

33

but the woman's grandson wanted to see her one last time and I couldn't just tell him no."

"Well, you should have," she shot back. "And I still don't understand what took you two so long to realise that something was wrong."

Not wanting to see poor Pastor Green berated any longer, I rushed over to help him close the casket. He glanced up at me and let out a long, drawn-out sigh. "How could something like this have happened here?"

"Does it look like she has any idea?" Mum said, her voice growing even more agitated. "If I hadn't come up here when I did, every one of our guests probably would have run away screaming, traumatised for life!"

"Mum, it all happened so fast. I did the best I could," I said, hoping to calm her down.

"Yes? Well your best clearly wasn't good enough," she said, before turning towards the grandson who had come back, his hand firmly clamped over his mouth and his eyes as wide as saucers. "I'm so sorry that you had to witness such a tragic sight."

Mum exited the now-closed curtain followed by the grandson. Moments later, I could hear her speaking to the guests, but I chose to remain by the casket with Pastor Green and the victim. There would soon be a police investigation, so I wanted to make sure that nobody touched or moved the coffin until they arrived to secure it.

"What do you think happened?" Pastor Green asked in a subdued tone.

I think he was talking to himself more than anything, and I struggled for the words to answer him. When I finally was able to reply, my words were jumbled. "I don't know, um, err. I, err, suppose someone must have followed her here or something. None of this really makes any sense, though."

"It will in time, Laurel," he said, patting my shoulder. "It will in time."

Just then, I heard the sound of sirens. My mother was still speaking at the podium, but even her persona was drowned out by the noise of the incoming police. My chest tightened as the sirens got louder and closer. I had not signed up for any of this. I only wanted to be back in town for a month or so for my father's funeral, but that had all gone right down the toilet. And now, everything seemed to be getting even worse.

CHAPTER 4

I remember how cold it was that morning as we stood there, waiting for the cops to show up to question us and provide some answers. The casket was now closed in an attempt to shield everyone from its gruesome contents, but the damage had probably already been done. I've been around death and decay most of my life, but for the guests there that day, it must have been an unforgettable experience. The horror in their eyes testified loudly as to how they felt.

When the police finally showed up, the crowd dispersed a bit, thinning out as the police sorted through the potential witnesses. To my relief, Duncan was one of two responding officers. Duncan was married to my best friend, Tara. I had only seen Tara over the years on the rare occasions I returned home, but we'd kept in touch on Facebook and email. It was amazing how little Duncan had changed since school. He was still angular and tall, and the features of his face, including his warlike nose, just a little too sharp.

"Hi, Laurel," Duncan said, his smile as warm and friendly as always.

"Hi," I said, smiling back at him. It was more of a partial, forced smile, but I wanted him to know that I wasn't letting the situation get the better of me. Being back home was stressful enough. I had to stay as strong as I could regardless of what happened around me.

"We're going to have to secure the scene and have the coroner come down to make a ruling on the death. He's already been called, but the faster we can clear the guests out of here, the easier his job will be," he said, pulling out a notepad from his pocket. He turned to the other officer. "Bryan, if you could go around and interview the mourners, I'll start questioning Laurel and the others who work here."

Bryan nodded and then headed over to the first group of funeral goers. I watched him carefully, hoping to overhear anything that was said, but

Duncan pulled my attention back to him. "I know that some of these questions might sound a bit accusatory, but it's all routine. I promise."

"Yes, I know," I said, pulling at a lock of my hair and twisting it frantically. I didn't even notice at first until he pointed it out.

"There's no need to be nervous, but I can understand why you would be. Let's get these questions over with, though. First, where were you this morning between about seven a.m. and ten a.m.?" His voice was stern and official all of a sudden.

I swallowed the lump in my throat, but it didn't do much to relieve the tension building up. "Uh, I was in the funeral home, in the office, getting the paperwork and everything ready for Mrs Forrest's memorial service. The casket was ready. No one had touched it since last night when Janet finished up with it. I checked on the elderly woman myself and there was no other body in there with her. I'm sure of it."

Duncan showed no signs of emotion, his pen scribbling into his pad like nothing else in the world mattered right then. After several long seconds, he looked up and smiled again. "Okay, and did you hear anything last night or this morning?"

"Not a peep," I told him, which was the complete truth. With the house being so close to the funeral home, it made no sense that someone would sneak in, dump a body, and then disappear without being heard or seen at all. Before I could say any more, I heard an unfamiliar voice heckling someone nearby.

When Duncan spoke again, however, I forgot about it. "Interesting," he said. "Well, the victim is a young girl by the name of Tiffany Hunter. She works, err, worked, just down the road at the café. Her boss says she went on a delivery and never returned. I can't go into too much detail, but we have reason to believe that she came here for that delivery, and then never made it out alive. Did you see her at all today, before the funeral procession?"

Thinking back to that morning, I couldn't quite remember it as clearly as I had hoped. "Honestly, I don't remember seeing her at all. I do remember that Janet said she found a tray of cold coffee this morning, though."

Duncan sighed, and looked back up from his notepad. "Can you check to see if any of your carving knives are missing?"

I shook my head. "There are no carving knives here at the funeral home. We only use butter knives and cake knives, that sort of thing. We don't serve meals here, just finger food."

"So the knife you saw in the victim," Duncan said patiently, "you have no knives of that sort?"

"No, absolutely not."

"Okay, so you and none of your workers have touched the body, correct?"

"That is correct," I said, but just then a strange voice yelled out behind me. I turned quickly to see the face of a young woman inches from my own.

"Hello?" the girl said, walking over to Duncan and poking at him repeatedly with her finger. I had to do a double-take when I realised that he was completely oblivious to what she was doing.

"All right, well thank you for your time, Laurel," Duncan said. "Bryan looks to be speaking with your mother now, so I'm going to help him finish that up, and then I'll speak to some of the others." He walked over towards my mother and his partner.

The young girl moved to follow him, but then turned back to me and scowled. "What about you? Can you see me?"

For a moment, my hands grew sweaty and my heart fell into my stomach. I swallowed hard, unsure of how else to respond.

"You can! You can see me, can't you?" she yelled again.

The last thing I needed with the cops wandering around was to speak to someone that only I could see. Ignoring her as best I could, I made my way over to my mother to see how her questioning was going. When I stepped beside Mum, I wished I hadn't.

"Yes, it *is* a shame, Bryan, but at least Miss Hunter is now in a better place. She's in heaven with God, right where we all belong. I have the assurance of that as she always attended our church. Now, I haven't seen you in church lately. Will I be seeing you there this Sunday?"

"Hey, you! Stop ignoring me! I can tell that you can hear what I'm saying," the voice said, whispering in my ear.

I turned towards the girl, who looked beautiful and young, but right away I knew that was all just an illusion. Now she was ageless, a ghost, just like Ernie before her. "Yes, I can see you," I whispered, shielding my mouth with one hand so my mother couldn't overhear, and pretending I was stifling a sneeze, "but we can't talk here."

"Wait, what do you mean? And why can't anyone else seem to hear or see me?" the girl asked, clearly unconcerned that I did not want to talk to her. "Is this all some sort of joke against me? And why are the police here? I saw a commotion over near the casket, but there were too many heads in my way to see exactly what was going on. What happened?"

It was becoming obvious that she was not going to let up until she got some answers, but how could I explain to her that she was dead without earning awkward stares from my mother and everyone else, including the cops? It certainly wouldn't be an easy task.

"Laurel, what are you doing standing around uselessly like that, you lazy girl? I'm sure there are more important things that you're needed for right now," my mother said, glaring at me the same way she always did when she was disappointed.

"That's okay, Mrs Bay, I actually have a few more questions for Laurel before we wrap up our investigation. The coroner just arrived, so you folks should be able to get back to business soon enough," Duncan said, offering me a reprieve.

"Oh no, what does he want now?" Tiffany said, combing through her hair with her fingers. I looked at her curiously, but it seemed to offend her more than anything else. "What? I just like to make sure I look decent, that's all. Can't blame a girl for caring about her appearance, can you?"

If only she knew that her hair mattered very little now that she was in the afterlife. "Tree, up the hill," I whispered to Tiffany and again pretended I was sneezing. There was a large, shady tree just up the hill near the funeral home. I figured we'd be alone there long enough to talk privately.

"Laurel, could I have that word with you now?" Duncan said.

"Of course," I replied. Tiffany stood beside me, sighing loudly as he approached us.

"I'm sorry to bother you again, but after comparing notes with Bryan and talking to your mother and a couple others, I just had to ask a few more questions."

"That's fine. I want to help in any way I can," I said.

"You still haven't told me what the investigation is about! Did someone die?" Tiffany asked, her presence beginning to grate on my nerves. The last thing I wanted was for Duncan to suspect that I was communicating with an "imaginary friend", so I did my best to ignore her, but it grew more difficult as time passed.

"Janet mentioned that you signed off on the

44

preparation and checked the casket yourself last night," he said. "That corroborates your story, but it's difficult to believe that nobody saw Tiffany this morning. I'm not placing blame on anyone as such, but there's got to be something that we're missing."

Before I had a chance to think, Tiffany flew into a panic. Her words made little sense, but it was clear that she was finally putting the pieces of the puzzle together. "I'm dead?" she yelled, standing right in front of me as Duncan continued his speech.

She put her hands to her head and then ran around the room aimlessly. I couldn't blame her, but Duncan's voice was completely drowned out by hers. After the initial shock seemed to wear off, Tiffany grew quiet and then vanished. I looked around the best I could without making it obvious to Duncan, but she was nowhere to be seen.

Duncan was still speaking. "Well, when the coroner puts in the official determination and we get our notes in order, I'll probably stop by sometime to update you on the case. Again, we can't go into any details, but since it happened here, I'll keep you guys updated the best I can."

I smiled and nodded, thanking him for not making things even harder than they already were.

As I watched him walk off towards his partner, my mind drifted back to Tiffany. I hoped she'd gone out to the tree.

When I approached the lonely tree that stood like a sentinel over the funeral home, I saw that Tiffany was there. "Hey, got room for one more?" I asked, sitting next to her.

Tiffany's face looked blank as she stared off into the distance. It was like everything that she had known had been taken from her. She slowly turned to me, her lips barely parting. "Did someone kill me? Is that why nobody else would talk to me? Am I... dead?" Her voice broke.

Swallowing hard, I nodded. "Yes, someone did, and that's why the police are here." I tried to pat her on the shoulder, but my hand went right through her.

There was no reaction from her, so I pushed on. "Do you have any idea who did it? Did you see anyone?"

Tiffany shook her head and closed her eyes. After what seemed an age, she leant back against the tree and spoke softly. "Why would someone kill me?"

$\mathcal{I}$ hate paperwork. In fact, apart from accountants, I doubt there is anyone who does particularly like paperwork. When I met an accountant for my old job, he asked me which accounting system I used. He reeled off a few well-known accounting software programs, and then looked at me expectantly. My answer was "cardboard box." That did not go over well.

Paperwork is one of the reasons I had never been tempted to go into business for myself. Self employment is the holy grail of all the misery that paperwork entails. Everywhere you turn, there is a new form to fill, document to sign, or letter to certify. I could very much do without that.

Now that I had inherited the funeral home,

paperwork was a necessary evil, an evil I was forced to face. I could hardly leave the work to Mum. Mum has always ignored paperwork, and the consequence of that would be late fees, audits, and the possible embarrassment of having our electricity cut off in the middle of a wake. Even if she hadn't been eternally busy with outreach programs and Bible studies, I wouldn't be able to trust her to balance a budget if our lives depended on it.

And at the moment, our lives did depend on it. At least the life of Dad's business. *My* business. I was still trying to process that part.

I looked forlornly at the stack of unsorted papers on the table in front of me. I was already arranging wakes, consoling the living, and playing twenty questions with a ghost whose death had occurred on my watch. There was yet another ghost telling me how to do my job and making puns about funerals. Adding paperwork to the pile was just plain cruel.

"Don't you have a secretary or something for this?" Tiffany sighed as she studied her nails for flaws. I needed at least one more cup of coffee before I had the energy to point out that ghosts don't chip their nails.

"I'll be happy to hire you." I rubbed my temples, trying to ignore the warning signs of an upcoming headache.

"As if." Tiffany gave a short, sharp laugh and rolled her eyes. "Let me know when you decide to hire a personal shopper. Your fashion is deader than I am."

"Ha, ha. Last time I checked, there wasn't a dress code for working at home."

"If only it were limited to here." The young woman gave me a long suffering stare. "You won't explode if you buy something nice. That bargain bin knockoff of a closet is a nightmare. The sequin tank top? You should have it burned and then buried in a shallow grave."

"I like that top."

"You poor thing."

Just what I needed. A ghost who was chief commissioner of the fashion police. I opened my mouth, but Mum hurried into the room, carrying a stack of file folders.

Tiffany glanced at me and then floated towards the door. The ghosts generally avoided Mum. There was only so much of her they could take.

"What are you looking at?" Mum's voice snapped me to attention. I turned my eyes back to her, realising too late that I had been following Tiffany's movement out the door.

"What are those?" I asked in an attempt to distract her.

"Some invoices and stuff from the past few months." Mum looked unconcerned as she plopped the box unceremoniously on the table. "I need you to take these to Mr Sandalwood, the accountant. We haven't filed anything in the last few months." Mum turned and rummaged through a drawer. "His address is on the fridge."

"Months?" I asked numbly. I grabbed the binder and flipped through the files to check the date on the most recent form. It was dated two months ago. I looked in horror at the stack of files with papers sticking haphazardly out of the sides. There was a Bible study flier in with the sales tax forms. I paused for a moment to look at the heading in bold, 'Will you burn to a crisp in hell?'

"Mum, what happened? Why didn't these papers get to the accountant?"

Mum shrugged. "Your father kept asking me to take them for him as he had so much going on, but I just can't stand the accountant." She wrinkled up her nose in distaste. "He's so strange. I think he works for the Illuminati."

I clutched at my head. "Where are we? What's been paid? Please say the bills are current."

"There's no need to be dramatic, Laurel. You always were a drama queen, right from the moment you were born." Mum put her hands on her hips. "I don't have anything to do with the business. You'll have to ask Mr Sandalwood."

And that is how I found myself, only hours later, waiting in the foyer of the accountant's office. I remembered Mr Sandalwood from years ago. He seemed old then, and so I figured he'd be pretty much ancient now. I hoped he was still as friendly as I remembered him, although I doubted he'd be any happier than I was to see a big mess of backlogged paperwork. If I wasn't absolutely terrified that we were about to be slapped with a flood of delinquent notices, I would have taken a day or two to sort them out before making the emergency appointment.

Back in the day, Dad hired the services of Mr Sandalwood's accounting firm, much to Mum's disgust, as Mr Sandalwood did not attend her church. It had been a source of ongoing conflict between Mum and Dad for years. Mum did not like to trust the funeral home's money to heathens, as she put it.

The elderly lady receptionist had probably been there for years, too. She was reading a magazine, and only stopped to take a sip of her tea now and then. I assumed it was tea. It could well have been brandy.

I yawned and stretched. I was the only one in the waiting room. I was early, so I reached out to the small table in front of me to sort through the magazines. There was nothing of interest: two financial news magazines, some car magazines, and some children's books. All in all, nothing to distract me from my boredom.

I turned to study the towering indoor potted plant. It looked healthy, to my surprise. That was the first office indoor plant I had ever seen that looked thriving. I reached out and touched it to see if it was real.

"Stop!" the elderly receptionist said. "Don't touch the plants."

I jumped back. "Sorry."

"What was your name again?"

"Laurel Bay. We spoke on the phone earlier."

The receptionist nodded absently and then took another sip from her cup. "You can go in now." Her head was already back in her magazine.

I shrugged. "Thanks." I wondered how she

knew. Old Mr Sandalwood hadn't called through to let her know I could go in, and I was still a good five minutes early.

I walked over to the heavy oak door and reached for the brass door handle. As I touched it, I was jolted by something, a crackle perhaps. It was like a low level jolt of electricity. I opened the door and prepared to greet old Mr Sandalwood.

The man who swung around, clearly startled by my entrance, was not the elderly, balding Mr Sandalwood from my memories. This man was maybe in his late twenties or early thirties. He looked as if he had come straight off a magazine cover for a young businessman's magazine. In fact, he was drop-dead gorgeous. I looked him up and down before I could stop myself. He was the best looking man I had ever seen, tall, muscular, with piercing green eyes and black hair. He had a great tan—a real tan, not a sprayed-on one. I shut my jaw and averted my eyes as fast as humanly possible. "You're not Mr Sandalwood," I said, stating the obvious.

"I am," the hottie said, as he opened a drawer and shoved something inside. "I took over the firm when my father retired."

I thought his move rather furtive and did my

best to catch a glimpse of the object, but only noticed that the sunlight briefly reflected from whatever it was. "Your father retired?" I parroted. I was somewhat in shock to be faced with a male model in a business suit rather than the ancient man in bifocals.

"Yes, I'm his son, Basil." The man walked over to me and extended his hand.

As I shook his hand, an electric jolt ran up my arm. I gasped and let go of his hand, none too subtly, but what surprised me was that he seemed to feel it as well. He turned from me and crossed hurriedly to his chair. "Please have a seat," he said over his shoulder. "You must be Laurel Bay?" he asked when we were both seated.

I nodded, and then frowned as a heavy scent wafted past me. It wasn't men's cologne. What was it? It seemed familiar in some way.

"You're early," Basil said, with a note of accusation in his tone.

"Your receptionist told me to come in," I said defensively.

Basil leant back in his seat and smiled. "Oh yes, Mrs Anise." He chuckled. "She was my father's receptionist for years."

I nodded, and then fidgeted as an uneasy silence

fell between us. I focused on the strange smell. What was it? Was it weed? It sure smelt like it. Some of the girls at college had taken to smoking a lot of the stuff, and their grades had fallen like a rock as a consequence. I was now more than a little concerned. Was this guy competent to continue as the funeral home's accountant if he was a dopehead?

Basil was the first to break the silence. His eyes trailed down to the stack of haphazard folders I was clutching to my chest with one hand. "Are those the files for your account?"

I nodded.

"How is your mother?"

"Fine, thank you," I said automatically.

"Do you go to her church?" He fixed me with an intent look and twiddled his pen through his fingers.

I frowned, thinking that a strange question to ask. "No," I said.

Basil nodded. "So you haven't come here to tell me that you won't be needing my services any longer?"

I rushed to reassure him. "Oh no, certainly not, nothing like that. As I said to your secretary, Dad left the funeral home to me. I've never run a business before, so I wanted to touch base and see where things are at." I mentally scolded myself then. This would've been a good opportunity to tell him that I was looking for a new accountant, given that I was fairly certain the strange smell was marijuana. I never think on my feet.

Basil did not appear to notice my hesitation. "Excellent. Well, I'll look through your accounts and then come to the funeral home in a few days to discuss matters with you. I'll have Mrs Anise call and set up a time that suits you. Don't worry, Ms Bay; everything will be all right."

As I left his office, I wondered if things would, in fact, be all right. How could I trust a doped up stranger with complex amounts of number crunching? *Perhaps the smell wasn't dope*, I thought hopefully. *Perhaps he has really weird aftershave.* Nevertheless, Basil Sandalwood left me with a strange, uneasy feeling. Something was up with him, and I had not the vaguest idea what it was.

CHAPTER 6

I was sitting in my bedroom, dreading hearing the knock on the door. It was strange to think of the room as my bedroom, since it was the room I'd had when I was a girl. Now I was an adult and I shouldn't be at home, but sometimes life throws you curve balls, and there's not much you can do about it.

Still, I had been thinking about looking into apartments. If I intended to stay here and run the funeral home, I couldn't live with my mother. One of us wouldn't survive the experience.

I could also move into the funeral home itself. The upstairs wasn't used for much more than random storage space, but there was a kitchen, a bathroom, and a bedroom. I could renovate it and make it work, but I would still be a bit too close to my mother. The same town was too close to my mother. There was also the fact that living above a funeral home made me a bit uncomfortable, which was strange, given that I could speak with the dead. Or perhaps that was the reason.

The knock I was dreading came just before six. That's when John was due, according to my mother. John Jones had maybe the most boring name I had ever heard. Surely he did; there was no maybe about it. He went to my mother's church, which wasn't a surprise, because I was pretty sure I was the only person who had ever been in her house who hadn't gone to her church. She liked her churchgoers, and that was that.

Mum had told me of the impromptu dinner date that afternoon. I knew she was trying to set me up and I had complained bitterly, but it didn't have any effect. I shuddered to think of the type of guy she'd try to set me up with, so it was with growing dread that I stood from my spot on the end of the bed and made my way downstairs, just as my mother was opening the door.

The man who stood there was as forgettable as

his name. Plain face, plain brown hair. His beige clothes were plain, and his beige shoes were plain. He wore a smug, sanctimonious, insipid expression on his pasty face, and he had the worst combover I had ever seen. I knew I was probably being hard on him because he was the kind of guy my mother thought I should date, but I didn't care. I had agreed to stay for dinner, even though when my mother had told me about it, my instincts were screaming at me to run for the hills. I had a pretty good idea how it would all play out.

"Hello," John Jones said when he saw me, and he put out his hand. I shook it. His handshake was limp. A couple up and downs, a very soft grip. I think I threw up in my mouth, just from all of the plainness.

I liked pizzazz and spice. That was me. I liked to live dangerously—well, somewhere between normally and dangerously. John looked like the kind of guy who ironed his sheets every night before he slept in them, whereas I didn't even own an iron, or make a list before I went to the grocery store. Yes, I lived dangerously.

"Dinner will be at precisely five-thirty, so you may take John into the living room and get to know each other," my mother said to me, and it was all I could do not to sigh and roll my eyes. I managed to control my emotions, and I led the man into the living room. We sat opposite each other on voluminous, antique couches, while my mother turned on the gospel music channel on the radio.

The uncomfortable silence stretched on for ages. John didn't appear as if he were going to say anything, so I started. "What do you do for a living, John?" I asked.

"I enter data into spreadsheets all day."

I stopped myself before I could say, "Of course you do."

"Interesting," I tried instead, even though it wasn't interesting at all. It was so plain and boring that I thought my eyes would fall out of my head.

"Wow, this guy is neat," a voice said, and for a wild minute I thought it was my mother, who had disappeared into the kitchen, even though the voice didn't match hers at all. I looked over to my right and saw Tiffany sitting across from us on an easy chair, her feet propped up on the coffee table.

"Not my idea," I said, before I could stop myself.

"What's not your idea?" John asked, tilting his head to the side.

"Oh," I said, looking back at him. "It wasn't my idea to have you over, but I'm glad my mother asked you." I thought that was a bit too strong, so I amended it. "You know, it's been a while since I lived here, so it's nice to make friends again."

"I was under the impression that I'm here to court you," John said stiffly, "not to be your friend. A man's friend is another man. A man courts a woman."

Across the table, Tiffany giggled.

"Right you are, John," another voice said, and this time it was my mother. "A woman is a helpmeet, not a friend."

"A help meat?" I said, startled.

"A helpmeet," my mother said, glaring at me. "A helper. Woman was created as helper for man." Before I could say something highly impolite, she turned to John. "I'm so sorry that my daughter is not familiar with the King James Version Bible any more. She's been in the city, so she must've gone over to new, radical versions like The Amplified Bible and things like that."

Both John and my mother screwed up their faces in disgust. I could see why my mother liked John so much. She joined us, sitting in the chair on which Tiffany had been perched, and I got to experience the ghost leaping up through my mother just as she sat down. Somehow I took pleasure from that. If only my mother knew that a spirit had just gone through her. It would freak her out.

"Do you work?" John asked me.

"I had a job in Melbourne, but it looks like I might be moving back to take care of my father's business now."

John shook his head, and my mother loudly clicked her tongue on the roof of her mouth. "That won't do," the plain man said. "My wife won't be working."

"I am no one's wife, and certainly not yours!" I said angrily, and would have said plenty more, but my mother stood.

"That's enough, Laurel," she said. "A woman need not control the conversation. I'll go check on the dinner."

I watched her go, and caught Tiffany's eye. She shrugged her shoulders. "So," she said, "find my killer, all right?"

I shook my head slightly, hoping John wouldn't see.

"What else do you have going on? Dating?" the ghost woman asked me. I slyly shooed her away, and then endured another half hour alone with John.

It was a relief when we were finally seated at the dining room table. My mother whisked the dinner out from the kitchen, setting food before us: platters of potatoes, carrots, and green beans. Mum served us all and then sat down. She and John spoke more than I did, and my mother steered and dominated the conversation, even though, according to her, that wasn't what a woman should do.

Halfway through dinner, John turned to me. "I'm out of water," he said.

I looked at his glass, which was indeed empty. I nodded. "Yep," I said cheerfully, wondering if the guy had a screw loose or something.

"A woman should serve a man," John said.

My mother knew me well enough to speak up before I did. I was half out of my chair, not to fill his glass, but to kick him out of the house.

"Allow me, John," Mum said, reaching for his glass. "I'm the hostess tonight, so you two get to know each other."

After that, I had even less than my already zero desire to get to know the guy. It was an awkward and quiet dinner, and when John tried to hug me at the door as he was leaving, I shoved my hand between our bodies and stopped him, and shook his hand instead.

"How rude are you?" my mother said after she shut the door.

I held my finger up, practically waving it in her face. "Don't do that again. I'm not interested in any men from your church."

"Well, I'm sorry. I'm trying to save my own daughter's soul."

"Mum, I would rather be tormented for eternity than fill up a man's glass because he ordered me to."

She folded her arms over her chest and narrowed her eyes. "You're never going to find a husband with that attitude."

I was seething. "I don't want a husband!" I said angrily. "And most certainly not a rude, sexist one like that!"

"Well, good, then you can work in the funeral home forever, and take care of yourself."

"I would love that," I said.

My mother snorted rudely, then turned and headed upstairs to her room. I gave her a few minutes' head start, and then went up to mine.

Tiffany was waiting for me. She sat on the edge

of my bed. "You should have fetched him some water," she said with a grin. "You know, to keep the peace."

"Be quiet," I said, "and I do hope you're joking. How long are you going to be here?" I sat down beside the ghost.

"Until you agree to help me," she said.

"While it's true that I can talk to you people," I said, "I don't run a detective agency or anything."

Tiffany sighed. "Don't you want to help someone who needs it, though?"

I felt too grumpy to have this conversation. "You're past help. You don't need help. You just need to move on. You're dead."

The dead girl with the long platinum blonde hair frowned. "Harsh," she said.

"I'm sorry," I said, feeling truly bad. "I didn't mean that. Sometimes I don't think before I speak."

"So you'll help me?" Tiffany asked.

"I'd like to, but I don't know what to do," I said honestly. "Watching *Law and Order* as much as I did in college wasn't enough to make me a detective."

"I just need to know," Tiffany said, sniffling. I hoped she wasn't going to cry—but then, do ghosts cry? I thought I was about to find out. "I just need to know exactly what happened to me," she continued. "I feel like I'm tethered here, and as far as I know, you're the only person who can see me, much less talk to me."

I sighed. "Okay, I'll do what I can. Can I ask you a question?"

"Sure," Tiffany said.

"Why do you guys do such weird stuff? Like haunted houses always have chairs that move by themselves, and shoes that get flung across the room. What's up with that?"

Tiffany laughed. "I have no idea. I'm a new ghost, remember? I guess some of us are just bored."

I laughed, too. "Back to solving your murder, I really don't know where to start."

"Hey, me neither, but I guess I've got all the time in the world," Tiffany said, and I grinned. She certainly did.

Just then my mobile phone rang and I slid it out of my pocket. I checked the caller ID on the screen, worried that John had somehow gotten my number and was calling to set up another 'date," but it was Tara and I happily answered. "Hey," I said.

"Hey, I was wondering if you wanted to come over for dinner tomorrow," she asked me.

"Well, it can't be any worse than the dinner

company I had tonight," I said, and when she asked me what I meant, I filled her in. When I had finished and hung up, I saw that Tiffany had gone. I knew she would be back. I had agreed to help her, and she was going to hold me to it.

CHAPTER 7

When I knocked on Tara's door the next evening at six, her husband, Duncan, answered. I stepped through the front door and was immediately enveloped by the same scent I had smelt at Basil Sandalwood's place. That surprised me, considering I was pretty sure it was dope. I had never known Tara or Duncan to experiment with weed, but I stayed silent, at least in front of Duncan, with him being a police officer and all. I thought it odd, considering it was his own house, but still, no one wants to be a narc.

Tara was in the kitchen cooking, and Duncan led me there. He left us alone, saying he was going out to the shed to wrap up something. Tara turned and smiled when she saw me. "I hope you like enchiladas," she said.

"I do," I answered. "Do you need help with anything?"

"I think I'm about set," Tara said. "Now if I can get him out of the shed again."

"What's he doing out there?" I asked. "Video games?"

"Painting," Tara said.

"Like what, flowers or landscapes?" I asked, surprised. I had never known Duncan to paint.

"No, little figures, little soldiers and things. He uses a magnifying glass, and he paints these little metal men, from various historical wars, and things like that. Sometimes it's knights and dragons. I'm just glad he has a hobby that doesn't involve drinking with the guys, I guess."

We laughed together. "Hey, by the way, what's that smell? When I came in, err, it smells like…" My voice trailed away. "I don't know. I thought it was dope."

Tara laughed. "Nothing so naughty, I'm afraid. It's incense. White sage, to be exact."

I nodded my head, feeling foolish. "That makes sense," I said. "I smelt it the other day at Basil Sandalwood's office. You know, the accountant."

Tara stopped what she was doing. "You did?"

I nodded.

"Oh." Tara bit her lip. I didn't see why she would think that information was interesting. Still, the interest was obviously there, and she seemed deep in thought. After a moment she snapped out of it and went back to her cooking. As she did, she teased me, a favourite pastime of hers back in school. "So what did you think of Basil Sandalwood exactly?" she said, a grin on her face.

"Oh no," I said. "I could have stayed home for this kind of stuff."

"I'm just asking," she said, but I knew she wasn't.

"Oh, I suppose he was very nice," I said, trying to sound as indifferent as I could.

"Very nice looking you mean," Tara said.

I wagged my finger at her. "I'm telling your husband."

"Telling me what?" Duncan said from behind me.

"How hot is Basil?" Tara asked her husband.

"Basil Sandalwood? Oh, he's just the hottest thing," Duncan said, and we all laughed. He had always been the kind of laid-back guy who could go along with a joke. The smile quickly faded from my face as he joined in with his wife. "He's single, you know."

"Oh my gosh, not you, too!" I fake screamed, and they both laughed again. Thankfully, the two of them dropped the subject for a while. Duncan ate quickly and then went upstairs to get ready for work that night. When he was gone, Tara pushed me for more details about the so-called date I'd had the night before.

"I don't know which was worse, John McSexist being there, or my mother being there," I said with a groan. "It was just awful. Think the worst thing you could ever imagine, and then multiply it by a million."

"What did he talk to you about?" Tara asked me.

"Why are you making me relive this?" I whined. "I told you last night."

"You didn't give me the juicy details."

"What juicy details?" I snorted. "Believe me, the details are bone dry. This guy is the driest person I've ever met. So boring." I drew out the word 'boring'.

By then Duncan had returned, dressed in his police uniform. He bent to kiss Tara goodbye, and then smiled at me. "Good seeing you," he said.

"You too, Duncan," I said.

"Stay safe please," Tara asked of her husband, and he smiled and kissed her again, and then he was gone.

"So do you know John, the guy my mother had over?"

"I've seen him around, but I don't know much about him."

"You do know a lot about most people here, though, don't you?" I asked. "I know it's a small country town and everyone pretty much knows everyone else, but lots of new people have moved here since I've been gone."

Tara laughed and cocked her head to one side. "You're acting mysterious all of a sudden," she said. "What's up?"

I paused for a moment, deciding how much I could tell Tara. I had known her since I was a child, so she knew I could speak to ghosts, but given the fact she was married to a cop, I couldn't really come out and tell her I was going to try to solve Tiffany's murder. "I have to run the funeral of Tiffany Hunter, the girl who was murdered."

Tara nodded. "I knew her. It's a shame what happened to her, the poor girl."

"Well, she was stabbed," I said. "And I don't

think there's a lot for the police to go on. Of course, you'd know more about that than I would."

Tara nodded. "Duncan isn't on the case or anything, but he said it was all very odd. He doesn't like to talk about work much, especially when stuff like that happens, so he didn't open up too much."

"She was attacked from behind," I said, "and she never saw it coming." Of course, I knew she hadn't, because Tiffany had told me that herself.

"I don't know. I know, well..." Tara said, hesitating.

"What is it?" I asked.

"I don't know," she said again. "I mean, I don't want to be throwing people's names out there. I'm not a cop or a detective, and I don't want to speculate."

I leant forward over my half-eaten plate of home cooked Mexican food. "Speculate," I said.

"What's gotten into you?" she asked, laughing at me.

"I don't know. Someone should help her. I saw her there, with the knife, and it doesn't seem fair." There was nothing enjoyable when you talked about death, and when it was someone so young, it was even worse.

Tara nodded. "How have you been, since your dad passed?"

I shrugged my shoulders and took a sip of water, so that I could make sure I wasn't going to start crying. When I realised I wasn't, I forced a smile. "I'm okay," I said. "Every day is a challenge. I suppose it will get easier with time."

"Is your mother all right?"

"You know her!" I said.

Tara grimaced. "She has her church. She would be getting a lot of comfort there."

"That's for sure," I said. "Most of them work for me. She got my dad to hire only people from her congregation."

"Oh, that's where Scott goes. I knew that."

Scott was the hearse driver at the funeral home. He had worked for Dad for about five years. He was a short guy, quiet and withdrawn, but he was friendly enough. He was awfully upset about my father dying, and I liked him because of that. He kept telling me my dad was a good man, and that he missed him.

"Why did you mention Scott?" I asked.

Tara clapped her hand to her forehead. "I'm an idiot," she said.

"What do you mean?" I asked.

Tara sighed. "I can never stay away from good gossip, I guess."

"Spill it, Tara." I waved my fork at her.

"He used to bother that Tiffany girl. Not bother her, as such, but he asked her out a lot. She always turned him down. I was going to tell you that earlier. It doesn't mean anything, does it? That doesn't make him a killer. A lot of people wanted to date Tiffany, I'm sure."

I nodded, thinking about Scott. Did he seem like a killer? No, of course not. He was just withdrawn. He could be so quiet he could be in a room with you for half an hour without you even knowing it. He could definitely sneak up on someone, though. I didn't like where my mind was going, so I forced myself to think about something else. "So, when are you guys going to have kids?" I asked, trying to land on a happier subject.

Tara laughed. "Whenever he lets me," she said.

"He doesn't want any?"

"Not right now. He doesn't think we have the money for a baby."

"I don't think you're ever ready to have a baby. If you wait until you think you have enough money, you'll never have one."

"I know, but he won't listen."

"He always was stubborn," I said with a chuckle.

By the time I left Tara's house, the sky was black. I went upstairs and found Tiffany on my bed.

"This bed looks comfortable," she said, looking at me as I came in. "I can't feel it."

"It's all right," I said in a soothing tone.

"What's with all of the Jonas Brothers posters in here?"

"It's my old room, all right?" I said.

Tiffany sat up. "Okay, okay."

"Tell me about Scott," I said.

Tiffany looked at me as I started to change into my pyjamas. "You're going to change in front of me?"

"You're a ghost," I said. "Turn around if you want."

Tiffany did so. "Scott? The guy who worked for your dad?"

"Yes," I said. "He works for me now." The thought of having people working for me still took some getting used to.

"Oh. Well. He was nice, but quiet. A little old for me, you know? He asked me out a lot."

"That's what I heard," I said.

"What about him?" Tiffany asked.

77

"Would he kill you?"

Tiffany's mouth fell open. "Oh em gee!" she said. "Absolutely not!"

"Are you sure?"

"Yes, he was so nice, really respectful. I mean, I'm sure he was upset when I kept turning him down, but he never got rude or anything. He took it like a man, I guess. He's a sweet guy, really, but there was just nothing there. Not on my end, anyway."

I nodded and sat on my bed. Tiffany had drifted to my dresser. She was looking at some old framed photos I had left there when I moved. It was really ridiculous how eager I was to get out of my home town after I graduated high school. I didn't take a lot of things I would have liked to have with me.

"You're fatter now," Tiffany said, pointing to the photo.

"You're deader now," I said in a grumpy voice.

Tiffany laughed. "Sorry. That was rude of me, wasn't it?"

I pulled a face.

Tiffany turned to me. "When you're dead, societal norms just sort of go out the window."

"What's it like?" I asked. Although I could speak with and hear ghosts, Tiffany was the one with whom I'd had the most conversation. I usually just tried to avoid them.

"I don't know. Everything is sort of, well... just colder."

I nodded. "My dad passed away. He's not here. He went on."

"I guess he wasn't murdered, huh?"

I shook my head. "No, he wasn't. He crossed over to the other side, which I'm happy about, but I wish I could talk with him."

"I wish my mother could see me, or hear me," Tiffany said sadly. "I go over there a lot, and she's so miserable. I want to tell her that I'm still here, in a way. But I guess, I'm not really here."

"You are really here," I said. "With me."

Tiffany smiled. "Yeah, well, thanks for helping me, but I'm telling you right now, you're barking up the wrong tree. Forget about Scott, all right?"

I shrugged. "Okay."

Tiffany started to fade.

"What are you going to do?" I asked her.

"Go push some chairs and throw some shoes, I guess," she said, and I laughed. She walked right through my wall, and I got ready for bed, wondering if I could, in fact, help her.

CHAPTER 8

$\mathcal{I}$ knew I could fix the leak. I stood on a small ladder in a room of the funeral home. It was a small room, not much larger than a closet. I had heard the drip while I was cleaning the cold grey room next door, where my father had once prepared the dearly departed, a job now left entirely to Janet. I had opened the door and been surprised as I stepped inside and my sneakers got wet. The water boiler was in there. At first I thought it was leaking, but then I noticed that one of the pipes running along the wall was damp and dripping.

I was deep in thought, wondering what to do, when I heard a screeching sound. "The wages of sin is death!"

I jumped and banged my head on the shelf. "Ouch," I yelled. I knew the words, 'The wages of sin is death,' repeated over and over comprised Mum's ringtone, but it took some getting used to.

"Shush, you inconsiderate child," my mother scolded me, before turning to her call. "Hello, Ian. Please excuse my daughter." She fixed me with a steely gaze. "That's right, Ian. We won't let the devil win," she continued. "Yes, we will both pray for her."

What? I was the devil now? I wanted to ask Mum if that's what she meant, but I didn't dare. I didn't even know who Ian was. Perhaps I'd be better off not knowing any of Mum's business. "Mum, I thought you were at a church meeting today," I said. "Didn't you say it was a healing service or something?"

Mum nodded. "Yes, but it was cancelled."

"Why?" I asked automatically.

Mum folded her arms. "A visiting pastor was going to take the healing service, but he had to cancel because he was sick."

I was tempted to say something, but thought it prudent to turn my attention to the leaky pipe instead. It seemed to be the highest one, so I found a rickety stepladder.

Mum had finished her call, so I asked her to hold the ladder still. When I was close to the pipe, with my mother holding me still instead of the ladder, her talon-like fingers in a vice-like grip on my waist, I was reasonably sure there wasn't a crack or anything. "Okay, Mum," I said. "The leak seems to be coming from where the pipe fits into another by way of some large circular thing. I've no idea what it's called."

"It's a flare nut," a voice said, and I almost fell off the ladder. I looked behind me, and there was Ernie. I tried to ignore him so my mother didn't think I was talking to myself. It didn't work.

"What are you looking at?" she asked.

"Nothing," I lied. "I thought I heard something."

"You did hear something," the dead man said. I didn't turn around. "It's a flare nut. You need to take it off."

"I think I need to take this off," I said to my mother, tapping what Ernie was calling a flare nut. I didn't know if he was right, but it sounded good.

"How are you going to do that?" she asked me.

"Twist it?" I said, but I lifted my voice at the end of the sentence so the ghost would know I was asking a question.

"Just call a plumber," he said. He seemed to be amused.

"I'm not calling a plumber," I said loudly, unable to stop myself.

"Well, now that you mention that," Mum said, as I climbed down off the ladder.

"No, I just need a gripping thing to take that thing off."

Mum frowned. "If you say so. Hurry up about it, would you? Don't forget that Basil Sandalwood is coming by at three to speak with us. Don't be late like you usually are. It's about time you started having some consideration for other people, Laurel."

Of course, I had not forgotten about that. Basil Sandalwood was coming by, Basil Sandalwood, the hot accountant. He was handsome, interesting, and didn't go to my mother's church. All in all, he was the perfect man.

"I wonder what he wants," I said.

"Who knows? His father worked for your father for a long time. Basil Sandalwood took over from his father," Mum said, needlessly explaining something I already knew to me for the hundredth time, as she usually did. "Unfortunately, Basil Sandalwood does not go to our church, and his father didn't either. I wanted Cyril Redwood to be our accountant years ago, but your father just wouldn't have it. It's not good to have heathens working for us."

"Mum, wasn't Cyril Redwood the one who was sent to jail for embezzlement when I was a teenager?" I asked her, and was met with a stony glare. If looks could kill!

I thought it best to avoid a lecture, and ducked my head so I could rummage through Dad's red metal toolbox. I found a spanner, and was keenly aware that Ernie was there. He nodded when I took the spanner out of the box and held it up, but I was careful not to stare at him too obviously lest my mother was paying attention.

"You turned the water off, right?" the ghost asked me.

"Mum, we should turn the water off," I said.

"If you think so," she said. "How?"

"Let me google it." I reached into my pocket. After a couple of YouTube videos, I had the water off. However, it was not as easy to pull the pipes apart, but I finally did. I didn't find as much as a hairline crack in the ends of the pipes. I attached them more tightly this time, and sent Mum to turn the water back on. I knew she had done it, because the pipe started leaking again.

I was almost in tears by the time she returned. "Just call a plumber," I groaned.

Behind my mother, Ernie was laughing. "I told you so!" he said.

As Mum went to call the plumber, I wound Teflon tape around the pipes again and again until I'd almost used up a whole roll. That seemed to do the trick. I headed home to take a quick shower and plaster on a lot of make up before the hottie accountant arrived.

I returned to the funeral home and went into my office, a big room near the front of the funeral home, where Dad did his office work and met with potential clients.

I opened the office door to see my mother sitting in my office chair behind the old oak wood desk, and Basil sitting on the other side. I was left with the empty chair next to the attractive accountant. As I went to sit down, Basil rose from his chair and reached out to shake my hand. I shook his hand in an awkward half crouch, my butt inches from my chair. I felt like I could just wither up and die, and not from the jolt that surged through me from touching him.

"The plumber is coming tomorrow morning," my mother said to me with a thin-lipped smile. She was the kind of person who always loved speaking of things that only one other person in a group knew about. It made her feel special, I guess. Basil just smiled as he waited for us to finish up with any plumbing talk.

"It's not a blocked toilet or anything," I said as I looked at Basil, and then I was pretty sure I would actually die, as his smile faltered a bit.

He nodded. "All right."

"You should have just done it yourself," Ernie said, suddenly materialising next to my mother. I was still looking at Basil Sandalwood, and for a moment I could have sworn his eyes flickered over to Ernie. But then he was looking back at my mother, and I was sure I was hallucinating. Surely, Basil hadn't seen Ernie. If he had, he would have run screaming from the room. I myself had a horrible shock seeing Ernie popping up like that, uninvited.

"So Basil, why did you stop by today?" my mother asked, folding her hands over one another and laying them on my father's desk.

"Well, I intended this meeting to be with your daughter," Basil said, pulling his briefcase onto his lap and popping it open. "I didn't realise you would be present at the meeting, and I have to warn you, I don't mean to embarrass you by what I have to say today."

That certainly had my mother's attention. I could tell she was torn between being intrigued and feeling as though she should be insulted.

"What is it?" I said, before my mother could choose and speak in response.

"Well." Basil hesitated, and then pulled a stack of papers from his briefcase and handed them to me. I took them, and he continued speaking. "Your mother has been giving quite a lot of money to various religious groups. They appear to be mostly televangelists."

"And is that a problem? Serving God?" my mother asked. "If you don't tithe, you're cursed! Read it for yourself in the book of Malachi!"

"Well," the accountant said, "it's starting to become a problem, given how much you're spending. If you wish to donate any or all of your own money, that's one thing, but you cannot spend the funeral home's money. It's not yours to spend."

He paused to draw breath, and I thought Mum would explode. Before she had a chance to open her mouth, he went on. "To be honest, things are in a downturn and had been for a bit when your husband ran the business. You're going to need to cut the needless spending, and you're going to need to bring in more business."

I glared at my mother, and Ernie faded away. When I turned to Basil, he was looking at the spot where Ernie had been, and I wondered once more if he could see him. Nevertheless, anger and frustration shoved the thought from my mind. "Mum, this is an insane amount of money." I jabbed my finger at the papers.

My mother sniffed. "It's a good cause!"

"Oh come on," I snapped at her. "Three thousand dollars to one man! Some man on TV! What do you think he does with the money? Besides, even if he does do something good with the money, you can't spend the business's money." I tossed the papers onto the desk so my mother could look them over.

She did so briefly and looked at our accountant, and then turned to me, her lips forming a thin line. "Well, did you come to tattle on me, or do you have any help to offer?" Her tone was rude.

I was reasonably sure I was going to dive over the desk and strangle my mother, but God himself must have intervened, because that was the only force that could keep me from doing it. "Mum, please be quiet," I pleaded.

"I don't have any ideas as to how to bring in business. I am an accountant, not a financial advisor," Basil said, ever the professional.

"We don't need to bring in business," my mother said. "People die and need our services."

Ernie popped up out of nowhere. "It's a dead-end business," he said with a cackle. "A grave responsibility."

I rolled my eyes at his puns, but then noticed that Basil suddenly seemed to be trying not to smile. Surely he couldn't hear the ghost?

"That bigger place in Tamworth opened up last year," Basil said. "It's a chain, basically the McDonald's of funeral homes. It ate into your business pretty well."

I sighed. "All right, so I'll have to do something to make people notice us."

"Make people notice us?" my mother asked. "Our business is death. We shouldn't advertise. It would be rude. What would people think?"

"We have to do something, Mum," I said emphatically.

Basil agreed. "You really do. Your mother needs

to stop spending the funeral home's money, too. You hold the purse strings. Cut her off."

I gasped and looked at my mother. Her face was so red that I thought her head might explode. She opened her mouth to speak, but no words came out. Her jaw moved up and down soundlessly.

I was so worried she would have a temper tantrum that I said the first thing that came into my head. "Okay, what if we do something fun with a funeral. What about celebrity funerals? What if someone who died was an Elvis fan? We could dress him up like Elvis and play Elvis songs. Surely there's a market for people who would want their funeral to be a party."

"That's enough!" my mother said. Her face was white with shock. "Death is not fun."

"We need to do something," I said plaintively.

"Death is death!" my mother said. "Jesus is calling us home, but those left behind mourn. They don't throw a party. Why, the whole idea is disgusting. It's a mockery!"

I sighed.

"Hey, I like the idea," Basil said.

My mother stood up and huffed. She hurried out of the room, dabbing at her eyes with one of her white handkerchiefs. "You ungrateful child," she said just before she vanished through the door.

"It's certainly something to consider," I said with a shrug.

"Really," Basil said, "you need to keep your mother away from the money."

"All right, I will. How bad is it?"

"It's bad, but it'll get worse. You need to figure something out to make sure she gets her hands off the bank account." He stood up.

"Oh gosh." I rubbed my temples and then stood up, too. Mum loved to spend. She went to the grocery store every day and bought enough food for a family. I have no idea where it all went. "Thanks for your help, Basil."

"You're welcome," the most handsome man in the world said. He smiled at me, and I melted into a puddle.

CHAPTER 9

*I*t was Tiffany's funeral. We had a viewing in the morning, and at noon she left, headed to the graveyard in the back of Scott's hearse. I drove along at the back of the funeral procession, with my mother in the passenger seat of my car.

Scott had not made an appearance at the viewing. He had stayed outside, near his car. It was plain to me that he had been crying all morning. I had seen his red-rimmed eyes when he opened the door for the pallbearers.

The trip to the cemetery was a short one. I stood by and watched Scott open the door once more, and the pallbearers took Tiffany's casket to her grave. I observed the people as the funeral went on. There were fold-out chairs set up along the grave, and most sat there, but I stood back, as my father had always done to avoid intruding on a family's grief.

The sight of Tiffany's mother crying as Pastor Green spoke was almost too much to bear. She was nothing but a mess of tears and sobs. The young woman's father was stoic, sitting next to his wife with one arm around her shoulders.

I looked around for Tiffany. I had expected her to appear, but I didn't see her anywhere. I wondered if I would go to my own funeral—if I could, when the time came—but I couldn't decide. It would be something to see who showed up, and who was upset, but if I died young and was murdered, I wouldn't want to watch my loved ones cry. Perhaps it would be different if I died peacefully at the age of ninety.

Scott was standing a bit behind me, next to a tree. He was wearing the same suit he always did when he worked, and tears were falling freely from his eyes. He saw me looking at him and nodded at me. I turned my attention back to the others, not wanting to make him feel awkward.

Tiffany's boss was sitting in the back row of the chairs, and from my angle I could just make out his face. He was around twenty years her senior, with greying hair, but he was fit and handsome. His face was simply a mask of pain, and it caught me by surprise. From the little I'd heard about Tiffany, she wasn't a very good employee. She'd called in sick on numerous occasions, and was often late. But here her boss was, sitting next to a woman I assumed was his wife, and he was holding back his tears. I supposed on reflection that it was most likely normal behaviour. Just because someone wasn't a model employee, it didn't mean you wouldn't care if they died. That man had worked with Tiffany every day for a couple of years. Certainly her sudden and horrible death would affect him.

If there was one person I expected to be very upset, it was Danny, Tiffany's boyfriend. I had been told that they had been dating for three years, and from everything I'd heard, it was serious and on the road to marriage. Yet, as I looked the man over, I didn't get that feeling at all. He sat with someone I took to be his mother, an older woman. She was crying, her face buried in a tiny handkerchief, but Danny was sitting still, impassive, looking bored. He was watching Pastor Green speak, but I doubted very much that he really heard a word he said.

As I watched Danny, my mother walked over to

me. She had been standing closer to the proceedings, but when she noticed me, she came over and spoke in a low tone. "You must have taken notes from your father," she said, indicating my position.

I nodded. "I came to enough of these with him."

"It's so sad, isn't it? It's never easy, but a young girl like this…" My mother shook her head.

"It's terrible," I agreed.

"Is that her boyfriend?" Mum pointed to Danny.

I nodded my head slightly. "Yes."

"Next to the woman wearing all the makeup?"

I was horrified. "Shush, Mum!"

"They can't hear me," my mother said in a booming voice. "I tell you, that woman's makeup is too thick!"

People turned to look at us. I hurriedly walked away from the gathering, so that my mother would follow me. She often spoke too loudly. I had been embarrassed more times than I could remember by her pointing out the faults of others at the top of her lungs, while at the same time insisting that they couldn't hear her.

I took Mum back to the funeral home to

prepare the coffee, tea and light lunch for the funeral attendees. Mum complained about the pastor's funeral sermon the whole way. "Pastor Green should've invited all those people to my church," she said.

"Mum, I'm sure most of those people do go to church."

My mother shook her head. "Not *my* church," she said.

"Does it matter which church they go to?" I asked. "Or do you think your church is the only one that's right?"

"Of course not, Laurel," she snapped. "That's a terrible thing to say. How could you be so hurtful?"

I rolled my eyes and sighed, and then listened to her berate Pastor Green for the remainder of the drive back to the funeral home.

Scott followed us back, and parked in the garage next to the funeral home. I was on the porch when he came out. "Do you need anything else?" he asked.

I shook my head. "No, but you could stay if you wanted. I know you knew Tiffany."

Scott looked as though he was thinking it over for a moment, but his face darkened and he shook his head. "I don't think so," he said as he headed for the footpath. For a guy who drove our hearse for a living, I thought it was strange that he didn't have his own car. I watched him go for a moment and then went inside.

I was hoping to see Tiffany, but Ernie was the only one I saw. He was standing just inside. My mother was in the small kitchen of the funeral home, getting dishes down from the cabinets.

"How was it?" the old man ghost asked.

"Sad," I said.

"I don't know why she didn't go to her funeral. I went to mine to see which of my friends had a smile on their face. I haunted those jerks—you better believe it!"

I laughed. Ernie had somehow managed to get on my good side. He was obnoxious, but endearing at the same time.

"Where is Tiffany?" I asked quietly. I didn't want my mother to hear me talking.

"I don't know," Ernie said. "I haven't seen her since this morning."

"Maybe she'll show," I said hopefully, and the old man raised his bony shoulders. I went into the kitchen, where my mother was unwrapping a platter of finger sandwiches.

"You know, John was asking about you at

church," she said.

"John who?" I asked.

"John Jones," she said with a tone of annoyance in her voice. "He came for dinner last week."

I had forgotten about him, in spite of how terribly sexist he was, given the fact he was so boring. "Oh," I said.

"He's a nice, proper man," my mother said.

"His name sounds like a super hero's name," I said. "Clark Kent, Peter Parker, John Jones. Except he wouldn't have a neat colour costume, it would just be beige or something."

"Why do you have to be so rude?"

I spent a moment thinking about the times I had heard my mother be rude to someone, even in just the last day, but the memories kept coming so I had to do something else. I made coffee in the machine, filled a couple of urns with water and then set about organising the tea.

When guests began to arrive, my mother went out to greet them, and I set up the food and drinks in the small dining room. I put down a platter of sandwiches and turned, surprised to see Basil Sandalwood, the accountant, there.

"Oh hello, Basil," I said.

"I'm sorry to intrude. I know you're busy, but I

wanted to show you this." He handed me a newspaper. Our fingers touched and sharp jolts of electricity coursed up my arm. "It's the Sydney newspaper," he continued. "It's not a celebrity funeral, but it's along the same lines."

I took the newspaper and unfolded it, moving to the side of the room along with Basil as some guests came in, no doubt drawn by the alluring aroma of the coffee.

"Wow," I said. Basil had handed me just one section of the paper, and he had opened it to the right page. A man from the outback had died and had requested that he be buried dressed as a crocodile. The picture showed a man wearing a crocodile mask and a crocodile suit. The story had made page three of the paper, and a Sydney paper at that.

"This is perfect," I said.

"Well, except that a man died," Basil said, frowning.

"Right, sure, yes, other than that," I hastened to agree. "But it says here that he even had a green coffin painted as a crocodile."

"I knew they sold customised coffins," Basil said, shaking his head, "but I never thought someone would actually buy a crocodile one."

CHAPTER 10

I stood off to the side of the dining room, smiling when people met my eye, and nodding my head softly. It was another page out of Dad's book. He was always present in the small gatherings we hosted, but he never made himself the centre of attention. As I was remembering him in his suit, his hands clasped in front of his waist, and friendly but appropriate smile on his face as he watched the mourners, my mother flew into the dining room, her face twisted into anguish as she cornered Tiffany's mother.

I had to fight to keep from rolling my eyes as my mother slipped her arms around the other woman, and held her close. She patted the back of Tiffany's mother's head as she forced her face into her bosom.

"I can't get over this," my mother wailed. "What a good, sweet girl she was. She went to my church! It just isn't fair. If there's anything you need, anything at all…"

It was obvious that my mother hadn't learned anything from my father when it came to the gatherings. She had never done anything like this when he was alive, but now with him gone, she figured she had full run of the place. My father had explained over and over to her that the best in the business made their clients feel as though they weren't there, while remaining available should the clients need anything.

I hurried over to the two women and put my hand on my mother's arm. "Mum, I need your help with something," I said.

My mother glared at me. Her thin mouth parted and she practically hissed at me when she spoke. "Can't you see I'm consoling this poor woman? Can't it wait?"

"Mum, I really need your help," I said. "I can't do it by myself." I knew that if I played up to my mother's sense of superiority, she would come with me. I was right. She stepped back from the other woman in a flash.

"Please excuse me," my mother said, and she turned to follow me out of the dining room. There were people all over the funeral home, so I opened the front door and stepped out onto the porch.

"I knew your father made a mistake," my mother started. "What can I help you with?"

"I lied," I said.

Her face contorted. "Lied?" she asked. "Why would you do a thing like that, Laurel?"

"I'm sorry," I lied again. "I just thought you were being a bit overbearing in there. That woman lost her daughter, and you were practically holding her hostage."

"I was comforting her!" my mother said way too loudly, sending three birds that had been sitting in a shrub in the front yard shooting into the air.

"I know, but that's not our job," I said.

My mother waved her hand at me. "Oh, you're too much like him," she said, implying that I was too much like my father.

"Mum, if they need something, they'll ask," I said in a soothing tone.

"Oh hush, Laurel," my mother said. "I can't believe you're so ungrateful."

I sighed. I knew she wasn't taking me seriously. My father had been able to keep her reined in, but she didn't see me as an equal. I was an adult, but I figured that was just how child-parent relationships worked. The problem was that I was now her boss. She held the mother card over me, but this was my business now. And that put me in a very awkward position.

"Mum, please leave her alone. I'm trying to keep this place running the same way that Dad ran it."

My mother looked at me, and I could see she was having an inner debate, trying to figure out if she wanted to argue with me. Thankfully, she decided not to pursue the matter, and simply frowned. "I'll go make more coffee."

"Thank you," I said, and I watched her go. Just as I reached for the doorknob, a voice called out behind me.

"Hey, Laurel, hold on a minute."

I spun around to see Tara hurrying up to the porch, her car parked at the curb behind her.

"Hey, I didn't even notice you pull up," I said, but it was obvious that Tara wasn't in a chit chat mood.

"Is this Tiffany's thing?" she asked, motioning to the other cars.

I nodded. "Her funeral was earlier, and the family and mourners are inside having tea and coffee," I said.

"Okay, I won't stay. I'm sure you're busy, but I have something to tell you."

"What's up?" I asked.

"Well, I know you were doing a bit of digging into this, the case, or whatever we're calling it, the murder. Duncan mentioned that the detectives had gotten Tiffany's phone records back, and she had been talking to her boss a lot. Like, a lot." Tara stopped talking to me and looked at me, waiting for my reaction.

"She did work for him," I said, somewhat unimpressed.

Tara frowned. "Yes, but how often do you call your boss?"

"I am the boss," I said, smiling.

"Well, before you moved back here. Did you call your boss?"

I shook my head. She did have a point. "I didn't have his private number," I said.

"Right," Tara said, clearly pleased with herself.

"And this was his personal mobile phone, not even his work mobile. He had two."

I bit my fingernail. "Did Duncan say what the detectives are going to do?"

"He only said they'll speak to her boss. Is her boss here?"

I shook my head. "He went to the funeral, but he and his wife didn't come back here after. It's mostly just family now."

Tara nodded. "All right. I should go, but it's certainly something to think about, isn't it?"

I nodded. "Yes, it sure is something to think about."

Tara hurried off, and once more I turned to the door, and once more I was interrupted. Tiffany was standing right in front of the door. "Can we speak?" she asked.

I looked around quickly. "In the house," I said. "I don't want someone seeing me talking to the air."

We walked across the lawn together. I opened the front door and stepped in, needlessly holding the door open for the dead girl to enter before I shut it. "I can't be too long," I said.

Tiffany sighed. "I know. I was in there. It hurt seeing my mother so upset."

"How come you didn't go to the funeral?" I asked, unable to stop myself.

"I don't know. It was just too weird, I guess. I might regret it some day, but for now, I just couldn't. I couldn't go."

I cut straight to the point. "So, I'd like to ask you about your boss."

Tiffany nodded. I saw at once that she looked guilty. "Were you were having an affair with him?"

Tiffany looked away and nodded again. "Well, he was having an affair with me. I'm not married, so I don't know if that can be called *me* having an affair." Her tone was defiant.

"You have a boyfriend," I said gently, "but hey, I'm not judging. I'm trying to solve your murder." We had moved into the living room. I was sitting on the couch, and Tiffany was still standing, near the doorway of the room.

"*Had* a boyfriend," she said sadly. "My boyfriend cheated on me. Well, I think he was cheating on me. There was a girl he met at our church. He said they were just friends, but I wasn't so sure. I would see him texting on his phone, but he wouldn't tell me who he was talking to, and sometimes he'd get calls and leave the room and stuff. It was just weird." She stopped and took a deep breath, or at least that's how it seemed to me, as I didn't think that ghosts could breathe.

"I was sure he was cheating on me, and it made me mad," she continued after a moment. "My boss is just a nice guy. I don't know. I know he's older, but he's so handsome and he always made me feel good, and it just happened. His wife didn't know. I wanted my boyfriend to find out, though. I guess I wanted him to be hurt. I wanted him to be jealous, but I don't think he ever found out. I left my phone around. I wanted him to pick it up and go through my texts, but he never did. He just didn't care, I guess. And I wanted him to ask me to marry him, but he never did. I think I really messed up."

Tiffany was crying, her phantom tears bright and silver, almost shining. I wasn't sure if she could wipe them away, and she didn't make an effort to do so. She kept talking. "And I was embarrassed. I know I should've told you about all of this before, but I just couldn't. It was embarrassing. I know you're trying to help me, and I wasn't up front with you. I just… I go to church, you know? I messed up, and it's embarrassing. I keep saying that, but it's true."

She looked at me. I didn't know what to say. The whole story was sad. I was searching for the right words when Tiffany spoke again. "You should go back," she said. "I'm going to go somewhere else. I need some time."

I nodded and watched her float out of the living room, by way of the far wall. I stood and took a minute to gather my thoughts, and then I headed for the door. As I walked across the yard, back to the funeral home, I saw two people talking over by the side of the building. One was Danny, Tiffany's boyfriend, and the other was a young woman. They were talking and laughing, and it was obvious to me that they were flirting.

I was most upset. I wanted to give him a piece of my mind. I didn't. I simply moved around the corner. "Is everything okay?" I asked.

"Yes," Danny said, winking at the girl. "We're just getting some air."

"Tiffany was your girlfriend, right?" I said. "I'm so sorry for your loss."

By the look on the girl's face, I could tell she didn't know that Danny had been dating Tiffany.

"You were dating Tiffany? You're disgusting," she said. She slapped Danny and hurried for the front of the funeral home. Danny glared at me and rubbed his cheek, and then he followed the girl.

As I made my way back to the funeral home, I

thought about Tiffany. I still was no closer to figuring out who had killed her. Danny was still my number one suspect, but Tiffany's boss had certainly risen a few notches. Maybe his wife had come close to figuring things out, and he needed to clean up the loose ends. I shook my head. No, people weren't like they were on TV, or in the movies. You didn't just kill someone, right? Just to get what you wanted?

No, that was a foolish thought. The only concrete thing I actually knew was that someone had murdered Tiffany. I just didn't know how to go about uncovering who it was. I didn't even know their motive. Nevertheless, I was determined. I wanted Tiffany to have closure.

I sighed, and then walked back into the funeral home.

CHAPTER 11

A couple of days after Tiffany's funeral, I was out to dinner with Tara and Janet. The dinner was Tara's suggestion, a girl's night out. Tara had invited me at work, while I had stocked supplies. Janet, the cosmetician, had overheard us, and since she was around our age, we had felt obligated to invite her as well.

Janet seemed nice enough, although I thought her a little strange. Nevertheless, I had been looking forward to getting to know her better. Yet as we sat over drinks waiting for our food to arrive in a restaurant, I was starting to regret that.

"People turn blue," Janet said, "and they get bloated. I make them look their best, but you just can't hide that fact that dead people are rotting. Gasses leak. Organs turn to…"

"All right," Tara said, lifting her glass up and interrupting Janet. "How about a toast?"

"To dead people?" Janet asked.

"How about to the living?" I said, exchanging a furtive glance with Tara. We clinked our glasses and drank. When we put them down, Tara started up a conversation. I suppose she was keen to do so before Janet had the chance to get going again. So far we had learned about Mr Gregory, a man who had been killed by a golf ball and needed an eye replaced, and Samantha Lyle, a woman who had died last year after choking to death on a chicken bone. Neither had been entirely pleasant conversations.

"I have some good news," Tara said. "Duncan and I have decided to try for a baby."

I clapped my hands together and beamed. "Oh, that's awesome!" I said. "What changed his mind?"

"I think he just got tired of hearing me whine about it," Tara said. "I don't care why he changed his mind, but I'm glad he did."

"You'll be sorry if you have a kid," Janet said unhelpfully. "You don't really want one. Kids are a lot of money."

I glared at her.

"I know they are," Tara said, taking it in her stride. "But that's okay, we'll figure it out."

"Kids, that would've been nice," a voice said, and I turned my head to see Tiffany sitting in the empty chair we had at our table. I resisted the urge to keep looking at her. Instead, I looked at the other two women at the table. Janet had her head down and was scratching the table with the nail of her right index finger. Tara, on the other hand, appeared to be looking at Tiffany out of the corner of her eye.

Was I going crazy? I could have sworn I just saw Tara looking at Tiffany. My friend held my gaze, as if she were daring me to say something. I looked away first. That was crazy—if she could see the ghost, she would tell me, wouldn't she?

No, because I could see the girl, and I didn't tell her. I figured a young woman appearing suddenly at our table would shock her, but it didn't shock me. It didn't scare me because I had seen her before. I had seen other dead people before. What if Tara had, too?

It was too crazy. I knew that. I tried to shove it from my mind, but then something else I had shoved aside a week ago came rushing back. I had thought that Basil, the handsome accountant, had seen Ernie. Clearly, I was either imagining things or getting paranoid.

"Girls night out, huh?" Tiffany asked. "I know, you can't answer, but I heard you guys talking, and it sort of makes me feel normal. I should go, though."

"No," I said suddenly.

"No what?" Janet asked.

"Uh, no, I forgot I left a light on in the funeral home. I wanted to stop doing that, so I could cut down on the power bill."

"I think I got them all before we left," Janet said, looking at me strangely.

"Oh good," I said.

To my left Tiffany was laughing. "This is fun," she said. "I could really mess up your day."

I didn't answer.

"I mean, eventually you'll have to tell me to be quiet or something, right? And you'll scream out 'shut up!' and everyone will look at you like you're insane."

Still I stayed quiet.

"Don't worry, I won't do that to you. I just wanted to get out of the funeral home for a while. I guess I've been sticking around because you're the only person I can talk to. Well, living person I guess, 'cause that old man keeps me company sometimes."

Janet lifted up a fork and was looking at it intently. "I heard a lot of things like this come from child labour in a third world country," she informed us.

"How awful," Tara said. She was really doing a bang up job putting up with Janet and all her Debbie Downer stuff.

Beside me, once again, Tiffany was laughing. "This girl is too much. I was with her when she was working on me. She put on a shade of blush that I wouldn't touch in a million years, but anyway, she's funny. She talks to herself a lot. Same old really, a bunch of depressing stuff. Maybe working with the dead makes you depressed. I know being dead can do that."

It was all becoming too much. I had a dead girl talking on one side of me, a girl talking dead people on the other side, and across from me my best friend, who I thought could see Tiffany. There had been that glance, but who knows, maybe when a ghost comes anyone can feel the sudden chill. I felt it sometimes. I shook my head. Tara hadn't seen Tiffany, and Basil hadn't seen Ernie.

Finally, our food came and our night went on,

passing pleasantly enough when we managed to divert Janet from her morbid stories. Tiffany remained for the whole meal, speaking every now and then when she knew it would amuse me, and a couple of times I had to fight the urge to laugh.

After dinner we all went our separate ways. Janet went to her car, Tiffany disappeared, and Tara was picked up by Duncan in his police vehicle.

"Congratulations," I said to Duncan as he rolled down his window.

"Does she tell everyone?" he asked with a smile.

"Just Laurel," Tara said, "and Janet."

"Who is Janet?"

"My new best friend. You're going to love her."

I laughed and so did Tara, which left Duncan with a worried look on his face.

"See ya, girlie," Tara called to me.

I waved. Duncan drove off, and I walked the short distance to my car. As I was unlocking it, a dark shape slid up next to me. A strong hand grabbed my arm. I swung around and found myself face to face with Danny.

"Who do you think you are?" he asked.

"Danny, let me go!" I said.

"Don't mess with me," he said, his voice filled with anger. "I don't appreciate what you did at that funeral home. You make money off sad people. That's disgusting."

I steeled my jaw. "You didn't look sad at all," I said. "Now let go of me."

To my relief, Danny released me. I watched him walk away to join a group of his friends who were waiting by the door. Before he went inside, he turned and pointed at me with a scowl on his face and hate in his eyes. It chilled me to the bone.

CHAPTER 12

$\mathcal{I}$t was our first celebrity funeral, and to I say was nervous was an understatement. The funeral home had a nice if modest speaker system throughout. It was commonplace during a viewing to have videos playing, moving collages of the deceased's life, and they were invariably accompanied by music. There were speakers in every room of the downstairs area, anywhere guests could go. We usually played soft, elevator type music.

Today, the music was of a different kind. The guitars were roaring; the drums were kicking. It was loud and booming. "It's just the way he would have wanted it," the deceased's wife said with a smile.

However, she was the only one smiling. The

others there, family and friends, obviously thought it was tacky at best and downright disrespectful at worst.

I was standing near the front door keeping an eye on the guests who were still arriving. It was six in the evening, and the man was to be buried the next morning. There would be this viewing, and then a small get-together after the burial in the morning. All in all, I had been able to charge quite a bit more for this funeral than others.

The widow had supplied memorabilia for the viewing. There was a blow-up figure of Gene Simmons, the bass guitarist of KISS. There were posters on the wall, and even KISS streamers.

I looked at the blow-up Gene Simmons swaying back and forth. It gave me the creeps as his eyes seemed to follow me. I reminded myself that the customer is always right, so I embraced the tacky kitsch, and found myself feeling rather proud of the whole ordeal. Even if most of the family hated it, it would be something that they would never forget.

There was even a reporter from the local paper present. He had asked me to keep up the KISS stuff after the funeral, so a photographer could come and take pictures for the newspaper. This was certainly going to put the funeral home on the map.

My self-satisfied smile was abruptly wiped off my face when my mother appeared. "This is disgusting," she said. "It's a mockery of death."

"Not everyone feels the same way, Mum. Some people want their funerals to be entertaining. They want people to have fun. Not everyone wants to be sad at a funeral," I countered.

"Well, Laurel," my mother asked me sternly, "is anyone having fun?"

I looked around. I had to admit she was right. Most people looked rather put off by the music and the KISS memorabilia around the rooms. It probably didn't help that in the open casket the deceased man had his face painted, all white and black and silver. He looked as if he could get up and go to one of the concerts at any moment.

"His wife is loving it," I said.

Mum's mouth was nothing but a tight line across her face. She folded her arms in front of her chest.

"Oh Mum, it's just rock and roll," I said in a conciliatory tone.

"I'm not stupid, you know. I know you think I'm stupid, and I know your father thought I was stupid. Everyone always thought he was smarter than I am. Well, let me tell you, I looked them up on the internet. I can do that you know, despite what you think of me. KISS means 'Knights in Satan's Service'."

"I think that's just a rumour or something," I said. "It's just an urban legend."

"Let me tell you, Laurel," my mother said, her voice full of exasperation, "you think you're so smart, but they don't just put anything on the internet. It's like a big encyclopaedia. It's all true."

What could I say to that? Not much. "All right, Mum. Well, even so, the client likes it."

"I think I saw her crying," my mother said.

"It's a viewing, Mum. You would expect people to cry."

Mum's lips pursed into a thin line. "It's too loud. God doesn't like loud music, or he wouldn't have invented hymns."

"I can turn it down a little," I conceded. I went to the sound system, leaving my mother by the door to welcome guests. I turned the music down more than a bit.

"Now *this* is a funeral!" a happy voice said, and I turned to see Ernie standing in the doorway. "Mine was horrible, but this one is fun."

"You're a KISS fan?" I asked, surprised.

"No, not exactly," the old dead man admitted.

"I just like bothering people, I guess, and there are a lot of bothered people here."

I shrugged. "Well, it's not up to them how this guy goes out. When they die, they can have all the boring funerals they want."

"Keep it up, kiddo," Ernie said. "This all seems expensive. Your father would have loved it."

I smiled and nodded. "I think so, too."

"I'm going to go now," Ernie said, and he walked through a wall.

"Catch you later, Ernie." I left the small media room and stopped to check on the wife of the deceased. She was by his coffin, reaching down and tracing her fingertips lightly over his makeup covered cheek.

"Are you all right?" I asked. "Is there anything we can do for you?"

She smiled and placed her hand on my arm. "I love it," she said. "This is exactly him. It's perfect."

"I'm glad," I said.

"I know some people hate it. Most of them do, I guess, but it just doesn't matter. I don't care. I miss him, and I want him to be happy, wherever he is."

"I'm sure he is happy," I said. "If he can see this, somehow, somewhere, he's thrilled."

The woman nodded, and she touched her husband's cheek once more. I left her alone.

Pastor Green usually attended the viewings. I was, however, greatly surprised when he arrived, given that he looked like a member of KISS, his face all painted white with black around the eyes. He had gone all out.

"Hello, Laurel," Pastor Green said.

I just stood there with my mouth hanging open. I wondered where my mother was. I would need to find her and prepare her, otherwise she was liable to have a heart attack.

Pastor Green did not appear to notice that I was rattled by his appearance, and kept talking. "Martin and Diane Harris have been coming to church for such a long time. I don't think I ever saw him without a KISS tee shirt on under his Sunday best. He played drums in the worship team."

"Oh, my word!" I heard my mother shriek from behind me. She flew down the hall and practically barrelled into Pastor Green. I was worried she was going to send him right out the door, but it wasn't open any longer, so she was going to have to break it down.

"You're a man of God!" she said in an accusatory tone.

Pastor Green smiled. "I am," he said. "It's my duty in times like these to offer comfort."

"Who could you possibly be comforting? Lucifer?"

The pastor laughed. "Diane Harris," he said.

"This is not proper. It's downright unholy," my mother pressed. "Certainly you won't have this heathen makeup on at church."

The pastor shook his head. "I will not," he said with a sigh.

Just then Diane Harris joined us. "Oh, thank you for coming," she said to the pastor.

Pastor Green patted her hand. "If you'll excuse us," he said to my mother. "Diane and I will go and greet everyone." He made the rock and roll sign with his fingers, index and pinkie extended, middle and ring folded down, held by his thumb. He stuck out his tongue like Gene Simmons, and walked off with the widow.

CHAPTER 13

*S*ince we had just had dinner earlier in the week, I was a little surprised when Tara called me in the morning after the KISS funeral to ask if I could meet her for lunch that afternoon.

The café was classic looking, long and chrome, with a spacious parking lot that wasn't as busy as I remembered it being years ago. I didn't see Tara's car, so I went in and hovered, until an old woman named Kathy yelled at me from the counter and told me to sit wherever I wanted. It didn't appear that she was willing to leave her steaming mug of coffee and the soap opera she was watching on a small TV bolted into one corner of the building.

I chose a table along the wall where I could look out the long bay window and see when Tara arrived. Kathy came to drop off a glass of water and take my order. I remembered her from back in high school. She had worked here then, and somehow she had looked just as old as she did now. I wondered if she recognised me, but if she did, she didn't let it register on her face. The only other person in the place, besides whoever was banging around dishes in the back, the cook no doubt, was a large man in a red shirt sitting at the counter. He appeared to be doing a crossword puzzle, given that his head was bent low over the newspaper on which he was scribbling.

I ordered a Coke and watched Kathy shuffle back behind her counter. The bell over the door chimed, and I looked up to see Tara walk in. She smiled at me and hurried over, dropping into the seat across from me. Tara ordered a glass of water, much to Kathy's obvious disgust.

"I miss sodas so much," she said, "but I'm trying to drop it so that when I get pregnant I won't have to quit cold turkey."

I nodded. "The things we do for kids."

Tara laughed. "Neither of us know anything about that."

"Well, I was trying to relate."

"Trust me, I'm going to need to live vicariously

through you," Tara said, accepting her water from Kathy who slammed it down so hard on the table that it splashed. She took our meal orders and then hurried off.

"I can't believe she still works here," I said quietly, when the old woman had made it back to the counter.

"I think she might be a vampire," Tara said with a grin.

"It would be depressing to be turned into a vampire at age one hundred and twelve, or however old she is," I said, and we both giggled.

"It's great that you're back," Tara said. "I've missed you."

"I know. I've missed you too." I thought back to her call this morning. "What's up?" I asked. "This sounded important."

Tara nodded and sighed. "I just wanted to talk. I wanted to clear the air, I guess."

I didn't know what she could possibly be talking about. Clearing the air? I hadn't made her mad, and she hadn't made me mad.

"I saw you looking at something that wasn't there at dinner the other night," Tara said. "Were you looking at a dead person?"

I smiled with relief. Tara was the one person

who knew that I could see ghosts, given that we'd been friends from an early age. However, we hadn't talked about it since I'd come back to Witch Woods. "Yes, it was Tiffany," I said. "She wants me to find out who murdered her. She doesn't have a clue who it was."

Tara bit her lip. "I'd almost forgotten you could see ghosts. We haven't talked about it in ages."

I nodded my agreement. "You know, I thought you could see her, too."

Tara shook her head. "I saw you looking at an empty space, and then figured it was a ghost."

"I knew I was wrong," I said, "but for a minute I thought you could see her. I must be going a bit nuts, living with my mother and all that. I even thought that hot accountant, Basil Sandalwood, could see ghosts too."

Tara looked startled.

"What's up?" I asked.

"It's probably nothing," Tara began, but after I shot her a withering look, she continued. "Well, you know how I'm a witch…"

"Yes, and that's something we haven't much talked about in years, too," I said.

Tara smiled. "Yep. Anyway, witches use white

sage for spiritual cleansing of rooms and stuff, and you said you smelt white sage at Basil's office."

My jaw fell open. "Are you saying that Basil Sandalwood is a, err, a witch?" I said a little too loudly.

"Shush!" Tara nodded to Kathy who was looking away from her TV and straight at me. "No, but the thought did occur to me. People who are into Feng Shui and stuff use white sage, too, so it's not just witches."

I scratched my head. "I wouldn't have thought Basil Sandalwood was into anything, not Feng Shui, and especially not anything to do with being a witch either. Anyway, wouldn't you know? Don't you witches have a special handshake or something?"

Tara laughed. "No, silly, that's Freemasons. I can't tell if someone else is a witch. It's not as if Basil has a YouTube channel or something. Look, he probably just has some funky type of aftershave." She stopped talking as Kathy was scurrying over with our meals. We thanked Kathy as she set them in front of us, and then she shuffled off.

"So, you really think Basil could be a witch? Or a, I don't know, a wizard or whatever? That's what they call them in Harry Potter."

"Not really," Tara said, shaking her head as she lifted her sandwich to her lips and took a bite. After she finished her mouthful, she said, "It's just that you thought you smelt white sage in his office."

I thought that over. "I can see ghosts because every firstborn female in every second generation in Mum's family can see them. Is being a witch hereditary, too? I don't think I've ever asked you that."

"Actually," Tara said, "there are people who learn to be a witch, and others who are born with the abilities. I doubt he's a witch, and if he is, he probably doesn't want anyone to know."

I tried to decide if I would want people knowing if I was a witch. I didn't want anyone to know I spoke to dead people, so I guessed not. I certainly wouldn't want my mother to know.

"So tell me about Tiffany," Tara said. "You said you were helping her?"

"I'm trying to." I quickly filled her in about what had happened, including when Danny had confronted me in the restaurant parking lot.

"He was there that night?"

"A coincidence, I think," I said. "He was just out with friends. But he scared me, that's for sure."

"I can turn him into a frog for you, if you want," Tara said.

I gasped. "Really?"

Tara had a fit of the giggles. "No," she said when she was finally able to speak, "but I'd like to."

"Me, too," I said.

"So it's him then, right? He's the suspect."

I shrugged. "Well, I don't know. She *was* sleeping with her boss. Who knows what's going on there?"

"Her boss seemed upset at the funeral though, right? Isn't that what you said?" Tara asked.

"Well sure," I said. "But that doesn't mean anything. If I killed someone, you better believe I would look sad at their funeral."

CHAPTER 14

I spent a long time in front of my closet the morning I was to be interviewed by the local paper, trying to find the perfect outfit. I wasn't sure if they would even take a photo of me, but in case they did, I wanted to look nice and respectable. I ended up choosing a skirt and blouse, with black flats. I was careful to apply more makeup, but even then, I ended up half an hour early. I went to my office to do some dreaded paperwork.

It was strange for me to sit in the office because I kept thinking of it as Dad's, even though it was mine now. It didn't feel right to call it my office, so I hadn't been able to yet. It still felt like it was Dad's, and I was just substituting for him. Yet I knew only too well that it was a substitution that would last the rest of my life.

As I worked up a final bill for the KISS funeral, my mind wandered. It was pretty clear to me that I was going to stay and run the business. What option did I have? As I thought things over, I realised that I had never actually made the official decision. It had just been a 'let's wait and see' thing, but I had somehow fallen into the reality of it all.

Ten minutes before the journalist from the paper was due to arrive, I felt a disturbing presence at the door. I looked up, hoping it was Tiffany or Ernie, but instead I saw my mother. If I had put some effort into finding an outfit that morning, my mother must have woken at four in the morning and obsessively slaved over what she was going to wear. To be quite honest, I had never seen her look nicer.

"Wow, Mum," I said. "You look great."

"Thank you. You look nice, too."

I smiled. "Thanks. Uh, why are you so dressed up?"

Mum frowned. "The paper, same reason as you."

"They're coming to talk about the KISS funeral," I said. "I thought you hated the KISS funeral."

"I never said that, Laurel! Anyway, any publicity is good publicity," Mum said with her best smug look.

I sighed. Of course, my mother would never miss an opportunity to be in the newspaper. I think she would even shake hands with Satan himself if he could guarantee her a five minute interview on national television.

"Mum, I don't really want you talking to the reporter," I said.

"What's that supposed to mean?" my mother asked, folding her arms across her chest defensively.

"It means I don't want you talking to the reporter."

"Oh, Laurel, don't be so dramatic. Why can't I talk to the reporter?"

I shrugged. "I don't think we have the same ideas on the business. I don't want conflicting reports out there."

"You know, my friends at church have nice daughters. They never speak to their mothers in such a way."

I felt a little bad, because my mother could have been right. I thought that I had been shorter with Mum than I needed to lately, mainly because we were living in the same house. I really needed to find my own place. I sighed. "Mum, I'm sorry. I just, you know, the KISS thing was great for us, but it's still tight money wise. This bill won't be paid and through the system right away, and we need to book some more funerals. We have nothing going on right now."

"Well, I guess I'll cross my fingers that more people will die," she said waspishly.

I rolled my eyes and was mad at myself for feeling bad just a moment ago. "That's the business!" I said. "I actually don't *want* people to die."

The front doorbell rang. As I went to answer the door, my mother tried to hurry in front of me, and I put on a burst of speed. We half ran, half speed-walked to the door, jostling each other like children. I got my hand on the doorknob first. "Ha!" I said. I pulled the door open to reveal two men. One was a short stocky man with a messenger bag. He smiled and introduced himself. "I'm David Baranski," he said, offering his hand. I shook it.

I could tell that David was the reporter, because the man he was with had a camera hanging around his neck, giving away the fact that he was the photographer. The photographer was taller, with blazing red hair. "I'm Ray Greenfield," he said, nodding his head towards me.

I introduced myself and my mother.

"This is wicked," the photographer said. I had kept up the KISS wake decorations like I had said I would.

"You and I agree on that," my mother said, and I wasn't sure if she knew the photographer meant wicked as in wicked good, or if she was making a joke. I had heard my mother joke less than I had seen her run, so I was confused.

"A man really had a funeral like this?" Ray asked.

David looked at me. "We could talk if you'd like, while Ray gets some shots, and then we can do some shots of you two as well."

I nodded. "That sounds good," I said. "We can speak in my office if you'd like."

David agreed. "All right, then."

I led the way, followed by David and my mother. There was no running like children in school this time, but I knew it was a race to the chair behind the desk. Once again, I beat my mother. I was faster in my flats than she was in her heels. I sat behind the desk and David sat across from me. In what was no doubt a show of immature defiance, my mother remained standing, near the door. She was frowning so hard I thought her face would crack.

The interview seemed to go well. David was good at his job, framing questions about my father delicately, and showing genuine interest in how a funeral home worked. I answered all his questions, and he nodded from time to time. Every now and then he asked my mother a question, and she seemed pleased to be included in the conversation.

"Just great," David said, when the interview came to an end. "You certainly lead an interesting life, and this is certainly the most interesting funeral home I've ever heard of."

I smiled.

David went on. "I'm sure Ray has finished. Let's go see about those pictures, and then we can get out of your hair."

We went back out to find Ray sitting on a chair. He stood up when he saw us. "Hey, this is the coolest funeral home I've ever seen."

I laughed. "You should have been here for the KISS music," I said.

"There was music?" Ray asked, his eyes lighting up like a child's.

"It was horrible," my mother chimed in. "You should have seen the pastor when he came by. I've never been so embarrassed."

"You didn't like the funeral?" David asked my mother.

She shook her head. I flashed her a look but I knew there was no hope that she'd be quiet.

"What did the pastor do?" David pressed.

"He wore that horrible make up," my mother said. "I don't approve at all."

"I see. Are you very religious?"

Oh no. David had managed to hit the jackpot. I knew I wouldn't be able to shut my mother up now.

"Of course I am," my mother said. "Deeply. Everything I do is a testament to God."

David nodded. "I see."

"Do you two go to church?" my mother asked.

"Mum," I said, but she was stepping forward, an accusatory glance in her eye.

"I used to," Ray said with a shrug. "My parents did."

"And you don't now?" Mum asked the young man.

"No."

My mother waved a finger in the photographer's face. "I see. So you don't mind the fact that you will face an eternal torment in the lake of fire and brimstone in Hell itself?"

When the poor man did not respond, Mum turned to David. "What about you?"

"I go to temple," he said. "I'm Jewish."

I didn't know how that was going to go down.

"Well, at least you believe in the God of Abraham," she said as she threw a glance at Ray. I wondered if my mother was mellowing in her old age.

"But it's not the right thing," she said, proving my thought wrong. "Stay here. I have something for you both." She hurried out the front door.

"I'm so sorry," I said, shaking my head a bit. "She's um, um...." I couldn't think of a polite term, so let my sentence hang in the air.

Ray seemed amused by the whole thing. I couldn't get a read on David. Mum soon returned with two thin books in her hands. She handed one to each man. "Take this, and save yourselves," my mother said. "I can't do it for you, so you have to do it. It's literature on the right path through life. You're both on the wrong path, like my heathen daughter."

David looked at my mother. "So will this funeral home serve someone who doesn't share your beliefs?" he asked.

I opened my mouth, but my mother jumped in before I could.

"No way," she said. "Death is about going to God. If you don't believe, then I'm not going to help you celebrate that, or help your family cope with their loss."

"I see," David said rather crossly.

"No, that's not right," I hurried to say. "We are happy to help anyone and everyone. We don't discriminate based on any factor whatsoever."

"Which of you runs the place?" David asked, suddenly interested in the conversation.

"I do," my mother and I said at the same time.

"My father left the funeral home to me," I said.

"I was working here before she was even born," my mother argued.

"Interesting," David said. I could tell he was taking mental notes.

"Uh, how about those pictures out front?" Ray

asked. He was clearly uncomfortable with the conversation.

"Fine," my mother snapped, and we followed her outside. I was suddenly nervous about the interview. In fact, I was dreading reading the article in a few days. Who knew what David was going to say about us now?

CHAPTER 15

t had been a long day, and all I really wanted to do was take a hot shower, lie in bed, and read. It wasn't even dark yet. I was pretty sure a sign of getting older was the desire to lie in bed with a book when the sun was still up, but I would have to leave a meltdown crisis about my youth leaving me for some other day. Right now, I was simply too tired to care. I pushed open the front door of the house, and stepped inside. As I walked up the stairs, I could hear voices. One was obviously my mother's, and there was another I didn't recognise. At the top of the stairs, I realised with some horror that the voices were coming from my bedroom.

I'm not a terribly private person, but the idea of

my mother in my room at all wasn't one I loved. If she was in my room, then she had something to complain about. There was no doubt about that. I had grown up in that room, until I graduated from high school and had to get out of it and the town. Looking back, I was pretty sure it had simply been an undeniable desire to get away from my overbearing mother. Hearing her in my room now, as an adult, I remembered the feeling well.

The door was open a crack, and I couldn't see my mother or her guest. I reached out and pushed the door open fully. My mother was standing near my small dresser, bent over it, motioning towards some candles I had there. A slim man stood with her. He was decades younger than my mother, with a thin moustache and black hair parted severely to the side. He turned to me when I came in, and I could already tell I wouldn't like him.

"Oh hello, Laurel," my mother said, tossing a glance my way over her shoulder, as if it was all right that she was in my bedroom.

"What are you doing here?" I demanded.

"Ian here had some concerns," she said.

"About my room?" I asked.

"Hello," the man said, stepping forward and offering me his hand. "I've heard a lot about you."

"From my mother?"

"Oh yes. We're great friends."

"I'm sorry," I said. He looked confused as to what exactly I could be sorry about.

My mother finally turned around to face me. "I do have friends, you know, Laurel."

"I assume Ian here goes to your church?" I asked.

"Of course he does," my mother answered.

"My relationship with God is the most important relationship I have," Ian said to me. "When you find the same, you'll be happier. I know your mother worries about you so much, dear."

It was strange to hear someone my own age like Ian call me 'dear.' I shuddered involuntarily. "I'm sorry, but you have no right to be in my bedroom," I said.

"You should respect your mother and not speak to her like that," Ian said. "If I had focused on relationships like that, perhaps I would still be married."

My mother snorted. I wasn't sure if it was because she didn't want me to know that one of her friends was divorced, or for another reason. "Ian, don't you fret," she said stonily. "It's not your fault

147

you got divorced. As undesirable as that is, I think you made the right choice."

I couldn't believe my ears. Years ago, when my mother had heard that our next door neighbours were getting divorced, she had taken them off the Christmas card mailing list, and had them barred from a church party that summer. If I remembered correctly—and I pretty much always remembered the stuff my mother said, in case I ever decided to write a book about her—she had said, "Divorce is the very worst thing anyone could do. It's making a mockery of God."

"Divorce is making a mockery of God," I said, turning to Ian. "According to my mother, that is."

The man's face fell and he nodded. "She's right. Another gem of hard truth from your mother. She's full of them, and I thank God that he brought us together in friendship."

"Ian's ex-wife was not a Godly woman, although she pretended to be," my mother added, "and that's all I'll say about that."

"That's all I wish to hear about her as well," Ian said, nodding.

I cleared my throat. "At any rate, I'd love to hear why you're in my bedroom."

"Well, I didn't see a lock on the door, so I

thought you wouldn't mind," my mother said somewhat defensively.

"I'd prefer you not to bring strange men into my room, Mother," I said with an edge to my voice.

"Ian is not strange. He's one of my best friends."

I sighed and rolled my eyes. "Why are you in my room?"

"I'm sorry," Ian said. "Perhaps we should have asked before entering your private area. I know how privacy can matter so much to those who have yet to find God."

I ignored his comment and turned back to my mother. I crossed my arms over my chest and glared at her.

"Ian has been seeing a woman for the last year or so. When they know each other, she likes to light candles. Ian was concerned that she might be into the New Age. I told him that you were into the New Age, and he came to compare the candles."

"New Age?" I asked.

"You believe in the power of stones and things like that," my mother said.

"The power of stones? Mum, I just like scented candles."

She waved her hand at me. "Regardless," she

said, "I invited Ian over to see if the candles were that similar New Age type stuff."

I turned to Ian. "And when you know each other? Don't you know each other all the time?"

"Heavens, no," Ian said, placing his hand over his chest. He looked like he would pass out, right there on the spot. "Only on Friday nights, after we listen to an hour of gospel music."

I glanced at my mother, and she too looked absolutely appalled. I simply had no idea why they were so shocked.

Ian went on. "I know we shouldn't know each other at all, but times are changing, even if Thelma here doesn't like to admit it."

My mother forced a laugh and placed her hand on Ian's arm. I cringed at the sight.

"Well, I'm tired. I've had a long day. I'd love to relax in my *own room*," I said. "Alone."

"I was just leaving," Ian said.

To my relief, he did just that. My mother followed him down to see him out.

I hurried around my room to see if anything was out of place, but the only misplaced items were my scented candles.

"Why must you always be so rude?" my mother asked me, upon her return.

"Mum, this is my bedroom!" I said. "Don't bring people in here to smell my candles. It's just too weird, not to mention downright rude."

My mother snapped at me. "You're calling *me* rude? I can't believe the way you spoke to Ian. Besides, we weren't smelling the candles—we were just looking at them, you silly girl. Ian's girlfriend, Sandra, insists on lighting candles when they know each other. He says she won't know him at all without the candles burning. She says it's romantic, but he's afraid it's New Age. She doesn't go to our church, you know."

"What on earth are you talking about?" I asked. I was beginning to lose my patience. "They either know each other or they don't."

Mum gasped, and her hand flew to her throat. "That very well might be how things go on with people your age outside the church, but inside the church, it's a little more than that. You don't just know anyone! You should only know one person your whole entire life."

"Oh my gosh!" I said, the light dawning on me. "When you say 'know,' you mean…"

My mother cut me off. "Hush! Don't you dare say such a thing! We don't need more filth in this house."

"More *filth?*"

"These candles! These New Age tools of the devil you insist on bringing into my house!"

"They're seriously just candles, Mum!" I all but screamed. "They smell good and make light. That's all!"

Mum's lips formed into a tight line, and for a moment I was tempted to tell her I was a witch. I wasn't one, but I would enjoy telling her that I was. Her only child, a witch. I savoured the mental image of her eyes bugging out of her head. I was snapped out of my pleasant musings by her voice.

"Ian is upset because he is already knowing the girl. If she is actually New Age, he will be due for an eternity of torment alongside her. You really shouldn't know anyone outside of marriage, but it is a different time, I accept that."

"You accept that? Mum, when you were in a busy supermarket and saw that the teenage girl scanning the groceries was pregnant, you left your things there and hurried out."

My mother nodded. "I was a different woman then. I know now that the girl deserved pity and guidance. I can change, and I have."

I snorted rudely.

"I live by God's influence, and I don't apologise for that," my mother continued. "And I never will."

"Mum, how come you think it's okay that Ian is, err, *knowing* this woman out of wedlock? You always complain about people 'living in sin,' as you call it."

A look of pure horror passed over Mum's face. "I most certainly do not think it's okay, Laurel! I think it's disgusting. In fact, I think Ian has got a thundering cheek! I'm sure that woman thinks he's going to marry her."

I was utterly confused. Talk about mixed messages. "Well, why don't you say something to him?"

Mum crossed her arms. "I'm going to. It's just not right."

"I have to say, Mum," I continued, "I never thought I would see you befriending someone so young, and speaking with him about who he, um, knows and doesn't know."

"He's my friend," my mother said stubbornly.

"I don't think it's appropriate," I said, enjoying myself. "And if I don't think it's right, imagine what all your friends and the whole church must be saying about you two."

The colour drained from my mother's face, and it was all I could do not to laugh. She was positively pale, as white as a sheet. She tried to speak, but just sputtered, her lips and jaws working but no words coming out. She turned on her heel and left my room, finally leaving me alone. I chuckled to myself and lay back on my bed, savouring my rare victory.

CHAPTER 16

*I*n the time since I had told Tiffany I would try to help figure out who had killed her, I had made such little progress that I almost dreaded seeing the girl. She never brought it up. We had struck up quite a friendship, which was a pretty strange thing to say, considering she was dead and I was living.

There was certainly an air of melancholy around Tiffany, an air of sadness that her short life was over, but I liked to think that I helped her with that. Without me, she couldn't speak with anyone. With me, it was almost like she was alive.

Still, I was failing her. I knew that ghosts were people who were unable or unwilling to move on. I felt awful about the fact that I had nothing to show

Tiffany about her murder beyond the fact that her boyfriend was a grade A creep. So it was a relief when Tara called me late at night. I was sleeping, after a long night of worrying about the funeral home and the fact that we needed money. I woke up to my mobile phone buzzing, a beeping ringtone and the screen bright. I reached over, blinked away a haze of tiredness and looked at the screen.

"What's wrong?" I asked groggily. Even in my low-caffeine state I realised that something was wrong since she was calling at a little after one in the morning.

"Nothing," she said, in a half whisper. "I don't want to wake up Duncan. Let me go out on the porch."

"All right."

I heard her move through her house, and then I heard the screech of the old screen door to the porch. "Hey, Duncan would kill me if he knew I was telling you this, but I thought it would help," she said. "Duncan told me that they caught out Mrs Kaplan in a lie."

My ears perked up. "Mrs Kaplan? Not Mr Kaplan?" I asked, doing my best to wake up fully. Mr Kaplan was Tiffany's boss. Mrs Kaplan was the wife he had been cheating on with Tiffany.

"Yes," Tara said. "They caught her lying in the alibi she'd given her husband. She was covering for him. She said he was here with her all morning, but turns out he was delivering coffee."

I shook my head. "But isn't delivering coffee an alibi, too?" I asked.

"Not a clue," Tara said. "That's all I know."

"Thanks for telling me." I lay in the darkness for some time, staring up at the ceiling. It was interesting that the wife had been lying, but I didn't see how I could ever do anything about it. Could I speak to her without raising anyone's suspicion? I couldn't see how. After ages trying to think of a way to get information from her, I finally fell asleep.

By morning I had made up my mind. I intended go to the café where Tiffany used to work, to spy on Mrs Kaplan. I had no idea what good that would do, but I had no other leads. I could hardly come out and ask her why she had given her husband a false alibi. I supposed most wives would try to protect their husbands.

As I was driving to the café, I glanced down at my phone and saw I had missed a call from Mum. I called her back on the car Bluetooth, but there was no answer. Next thing, I had a text. I pulled over to read it. 'Did you call me? This is Mum.'

I called her back. This time, she picked up. "Mum, it's me. What did you call me about?"

"Who is it?" she screeched.

"Me, Mum. Your daughter. If you check the caller I.D. you will see my name."

"Oh, Laurel." She almost sounded disappointed. "What do you want?"

I rolled my eyes. "I'm calling you back because you called me."

"No, Laurel, *you* called *me* just then." Her tone was exasperated.

"Mum, I only called you as you called me, and I'm calling you back."

"What's wrong with you, Laurel? You just called me. If you're not going to speak, I'm hanging up." She did just that.

I clenched the steering wheel and let out a groan.

My day seemed to improve when I entered the café. I was the only one there, so I took a seat against the wall. From there, I could see both Mrs Kaplan and the street. There was no sign of Mr Kaplan, only a waitress who looked to be the same age as the Kaplans.

When the waitress brought my coffee, I decided to be bold. "It's a shame about Tiffany," I said.

She turned to me and nodded. "Yes, it's very sad. You grew up here, didn't you?"

"Yes, I did," I said. "I was gone for a while, years really."

"But you knew Tiffany?"

"Yes," I said. Of course, I couldn't explain that I only knew Tiffany after her death, because I spoke to her spirit regularly. "I did her funeral."

The woman's hand flew to her mouth. "Oh, yes! That was where Tiffany was, well, you know, murdered." She finished her sentence in a whisper, and glanced over her shoulder. "The police keep coming here."

"How awful," I said in a conspiratorial tone. "I hope they don't suspect Mr or Mrs Kaplan."

The waitress sighed. I looked her over for the first time. She was attractive, but had a stressed air about her helped along by the deep wrinkles at her eyes and the corners of her mouth. She had an overdone spray tan. Her hair was dyed blonde, although the roots were beginning to show brown. "I didn't think the cops would buy the delivery stuff. No one was with him, and there's no way for them to confirm it."

"But he actually was doing deliveries at the time, wasn't he?"

She nodded. "Yes, but still, it wouldn't have taken any time at all to pop over to the funeral home. It could've happened between deliveries."

I was taken aback. "Do you think Mr Kaplan killed Tiffany?"

The waitress looked aghast, and shook her head emphatically. "Absolutely not," she said. "He could never do such a thing."

I took a sip of my coffee and smiled at her. "I hope they catch whoever did it."

The waitress shrugged and took her leave, leaving me disappointed. I was no further along with my inquiries.

Tiffany suddenly appeared in front of me, making me gasp and jump. Luckily, no one was in the café.

"What did she say?" she asked.

"I think I want to find out some things about your boss," I said.

Tiffany shook her head. "You're looking into the wrong man."

"I just want to look into everything," I said. "I want to find out who killed you."

The dead girl nodded. "You and me both, sister."

CHAPTER 17

I didn't know how I was going to verify the fact that Martin Kaplan had been delivering coffee when Tiffany was murdered. I was pretty sure if I walked up to him and demanded to know where he was the day that Tiffany was killed, he would probably call the police. The last thing I needed was to be standing in front of Duncan and his fellow officers, trying to explain why I had such an interest in Tiffany's murder. No, I needed another approach, but how could I confirm that Martin was delivering coffee at the time that Tiffany was killed?

I could go to the businesses that regularly had coffee delivered each morning, but how would I get the information? The answer came to me swiftly, but it was so obvious that I mentally kicked myself for having to think of it at all. Tiffany herself could be of help.

Of course, it wasn't always easy to find the girl. She was walking this world, unable to move on until she felt at peace with her death, but she wasn't always hanging around the funeral home. I thought that she perhaps went to check on her parents, in particular her mother, but I never asked. It felt like prying. Often though, she was somewhere in the funeral home.

I walked around the funeral home, but Tiffany was nowhere to be seen. I had to get to work, and figured she would turn up at some point. I had a few calls to make. Business was picking up. We had received a lot of publicity over the recent KISS funeral, as the newspaper article had turned out to be nowhere near as bad as I had expected. In fact, it was bordering on praising the funeral home. To my relief, David had not mentioned my mother at all. And thanks to his article, I had more messages than ever waiting for me on the answering machine.

The day stretched on, and still I heard nothing from Tiffany. I took a small break for lunch and went to the house. I made myself a sandwich and ate it while I stood at the kitchen counter. I wondered where my dead friend was. I really wanted to ask her where her boss usually delivered coffee. The longer I waited, the more likely it was that no one would be able to remember anything that had happened on that day.

I thought of one other place she could be, besides her mother's house, so I hurried to my car.

The graveyard in which Tiffany had been buried was rambling, with a rolling green mound near the centre. I pulled up outside the iron gates and parked on the side of the road. As I climbed out of my car, I could see her sitting in front of her headstone.

"Hey," she said. She sounded sad, and she looked it as well.

"I didn't know you came here," I said softly.

"This is the first time actually. It's weird, knowing that I'm buried here, right under where I'm sitting."

"That's just your body," I said. "You are you. You didn't *have* a soul; you *are* a soul. You had a body."

Tiffany smiled at me as I sat beside her. "I like my headstone. It's pretty. Is that weird?"

I returned her smile and shrugged. "I don't

know. I'm not sure how you should feel. There probably aren't any rules, you know?"

Tiffany nodded. "Why did you come out here?"

"I was looking for you. I need your help with something."

"Murder investigation stuff?" she asked hopefully.

I nodded.

"I'm sorry I asked you to do that for me. You don't have to if you don't want to. It was dumb. I just need to know, but the police are working on it."

"I *want* to help you. I told you I would, and I will," I said. "I like you, and I want to find out how, well, how you got into this situation." *Namely, dead*, I thought, but I didn't want to upset her.

"What do you need to know?" she asked me.

"Where did your boss make deliveries each day?"

Tiffany sighed and shook her head. "Still on him? I really don't think it's Martin."

"I know, but indulge me," I said. "He went each morning, didn't he?"

Tiffany nodded. "Yes, he usually delivered to the antique store, the hardware store, and the Kennison farm."

I was surprised. "Mr Kennison? With the farm out on Kingstown Road?"

"Yes. Mr Kennison has three guys working for him. He gets them all coffee each morning."

"Heck of a boss, huh?"

Tiffany grinned. "Mine was better. I'm telling you, Martin has nothing to do with this. You're just caught up on him because I was having an affair with him. Maybe you watch too much TV. It's always the guy the girl is sleeping with on shows, right?"

"Perhaps I am. I just want to be thorough, and if he was going all the way out to that farm, that should clear him."

"Maybe then you can leave him alone," Tiffany said.

"If it checks out, it checks out. I'm just trying to help."

"I know," Tiffany said. "I'm sorry. I asked you to help me, after all. But wouldn't the police have already checked his alibi?'

I shrugged. "I don't have a clue whether they did or they didn't. I have to do this by myself."

Tiffany nodded. "Okay, thanks."

"All right," I said as I stood. I wanted to put my hand on her shoulder, but I couldn't. Tiffany hadn't felt human contact in a month, and she would never do so again. The sudden thought made me sad. I hurried back to my car so she wouldn't see me cry.

I figured there was no point going to the places that Martin Kaplan had delivered to in town, so I headed for Mr Kennison's farm. If I could place Martin there around the time of Tiffany's murder, then it would clear him.

When I made it to the farm, I pulled onto a long dirt driveway, my tires throwing up clouds of dust as I bounced along. There was a large farmhouse at the end of the drive, and everything was surrounded by brown fields. I parked at the end of the drive next to an old red tractor. I climbed out of my car and went to the front door of the home. I knocked, but no one answered.

I stepped off the porch and shielded the sun from my eyes. I peered all around, trying to find Mr Kennison, but the fields were large and I couldn't see him. I went around the back of the house and looked. I could see a green tractor rolling slowly across the ground. I sighed and started to walk.

As I got closer I could see that it wasn't Mr Kennison driving the tractor, but a young man of about twenty. He stopped when he saw me and killed the tractor's engine. He climbed down and grabbed a water bottle from under the seat, and took a long drink.

"Can I help you?" he asked.

"Could you point me towards Mr Kennison?"

"Are you another cop?"

"No," I said, unsure if I should say anything else.

"Good, he's fed up talking to cops," the guy said. He pointed behind him, to a thin line of trees. "Wayne Kennison's out there putting in strainer posts."

I turned and left him to his work, and headed out towards the trees. Mr Kennison must have been around seventy years of age, but he looked like a man decades younger. He was strong. He had a broad chest, and his face and arms were deep brown, tanned after years of being in the sun. He saw me at once and stopped what he was doing.

"You're Larry's daughter, aren't you?" he asked as I approached.

"Yes," I said. I was surprised that he remembered me.

He pulled his hat off his head and wiped the sweat from his forehead. "Sorry to hear about your father."

I nodded. "Thanks."

"What can I do for you?"

"I wanted to ask you something, and it might sound weird, but I'm asking for a friend," I said. "I wanted to know if Martin Kaplan was here…"

He raised his hand, cutting me off. "That's what the cops asked me a few days ago," he said. "I'll save you some time and tell you what I told them. Usually, Martin did bring me coffee every day. The day that girl was murdered in town, he came, but he was about an hour later than usual. He said he had some car trouble out on the Retreat Road, and it took a while for anyone to get out to him. I don't know anything more than that."

His news hit me like a ton of bricks. Martin had been here, but not until after Tiffany had been killed. Tiffany wasn't going to like hearing that. As much of a jerk as Danny was, it was looking less and less to me like he had killed Tiffany, and more and more like her lover, Martin Kaplan, was the murderer. All I needed to find out now was his motive.

CHAPTER 18

I was at the Kaplans' café about to have lunch. I thought it a good way to multi-task. I needed to eat lunch, and I hoped that I'd pick up some information or observe something of interest. Mr Kaplan was now on the top of my list of suspects—in that regard he had well and truly gone past Danny.

At least that had been my plan. I was waiting for my order, trying to peer out the back for any sign of Mr or Mrs Kaplan, when John Jones appeared in front of me. It was all I could do not to groan.

"Hi, Laurel. Are you having lunch here?"

I bit back the remark on the end of my tongue,

and took a deep breath before answering. "Yes," I said evenly, willing him to go away.

John leant forward and looked me up and down, leering at me. "Laurel, if you don't mind me saying so, I think you need to dress in more modest apparel."

"I *do* mind you saying so!" I snapped. "Would you please leave?"

He produced some flowers from behind his back. They were wilted, perhaps even dead, yellow daisies. I thought I had seen a man hunched over the flowers in the tubs on the footpath only moments before. "These are for you!" he said with a flourish.

I recoiled. "Thank you for your thought, John, but I cannot accept gifts from strange men." I tried to smile. I figured it was like writing a cutting comment on Facebook and following it with a LOL.

"I'm not strange," he said in an offended tone. "I am a veritable pillar of society. Pastor Green said he will put me in charge of the coffee after church from now on."

"Congratulations," I said. I thought of my options. I couldn't leave, as my meal was on its way. Before I could tell him to leave again, I was distracted by a rather strange smell, something like a mixture of embalming fluid and cheap stale perfume. I sneezed violently. "What on earth is that smell?" I said, after I had excused myself for sneezing.

John beamed. "It's my men's cologne," he said. "Do you like it?"

There was no polite way to answer that. As I was deciding what to say, John continued. "I haven't seen you at church, Laurel. Will we see you there next week?"

"No," I said forcefully. "You won't."

To my dismay, John did not appear to be discouraged. "I cannot date a woman who does not attend the church, Laurel..." he began, but I cut him off.

"John, I don't mean to be rude, but I am never going to date you. *Never.* Do you understand?"

John smiled thinly. "Your mother said you would play hard to get. Laurel, I must tell you that I am typical of a good Christian man. I am *in* the world, but I am not *of* this world. I do not play the games that the unchurched women of the world with their worldly ways do."

Okay, time to take off the gloves. I was about to say something immensely rude when John edged himself towards the chair opposite me. I watched with horror as he made to lower himself onto it.

"No!" I said, holding up a hand.

"Sorry I'm late," a male voice said.

I looked up with great relief to see Basil Sandalwood. He whisked the chair out from under John Jones. John almost fell and had to clutch the table to support himself.

Basil looked at John. "And you are?" he said.

John cowered. "John Jones," he stammered in a weak voice.

"John is my *mother's* friend from her church," I said.

"I'm Basil Sandalwood," Basil said to John.

John nodded and then scurried away to a nearby table, and sat facing me.

"Thanks for rescuing me," I whispered to Basil. As our eyes met, a weird feeling came over me. It was like a minor electric shock, or a moment of precognition. It passed within a nanosecond.

Basil smiled. "No problem. I could hear what he was saying to you, so I figured you needed some help."

"That's for sure!" I said loudly, glaring at John, who was fixated on staring at me and seemed to be straining to overhear the conversation. "Thanks again. I didn't even see you there."

Basil chuckled. "Well, you were somewhat distracted." He broke off to order coffee, and then turned his attention back to me. "So, do you like being back in Witch Woods? Or do you miss the city?"

I shrugged. "I do miss the city, and I thought I'd hate being back here, but I'm beginning to like it now. Everyone's so friendly." I stopped speaking and shot a look at John Jones. "Well, some are *too* friendly."

The waitress returned with our orders, my meal and Basil's coffee. She looked appraisingly at Basil, and my stomach clenched with a pang of jealousy. The café was not far from his office, so I figured he'd be in there often. Anyway, what was wrong with me? It wasn't as if we were dating.

At any rate, Basil appeared to be unaware of the waitress's scrutiny. "What's the story with that guy?" he said, nodding in John's direction.

I groaned. "Mum tried to set me up with him. She invited him over to dinner and tried to push me onto him."

Basil nodded. "Your mother can be quite persistent, if you don't mind me saying so. I'm surprised she allowed your father to use Dad's accounting firm for all those years."

"Me, too," I said with a laugh. "She doesn't approve of anyone who doesn't go to her church."

"By the way," Basil said, "I have a new business card." He reached in his wallet, and as he did so, a little piece of crystal fell out. He grabbed it like lightning and shoved it back in his wallet, and then handed me his business card.

"What was that crystal?" I asked, even though I knew it was none of my business.

A slow red flush travelled up Basil's face. For a moment I thought he was going to deny having it, but after a lengthy pause, he finally said, "It's citrine."

"Citrine?" I parroted.

"Yes," he said.

It was clear to me that Basil wasn't going to tell me why the citrine was in his wallet, but I already had a good idea. "I've heard something about keeping a piece of citrine near your money to increase wealth," I said.

Basil turned a deeper shade of red. "Err, yes," he said. "I suppose you think that's a silly idea."

I laughed. "Not at all. You'd be surprised what I

believe in. I think it's a good idea. I should get myself a piece of the stuff."

Basil appeared taken aback by my remark. "Not many people in Witch Woods would approve of me being into crystals. Most people go to your mother's church."

I grimaced. "Yes, Mum hates crystals, and candles, too. She had a fit that I have candles in my room. I must say, it's funny to hear an accountant come out with such a statement about crystals."

Basil simply shrugged. "I'm quite open-minded about spiritual matters." He fixed me with a gaze at that point, as if he wanted me to respond in a certain way.

"Me, too," I said lamely, not knowing what else to say. After all, I was indeed open-minded about spiritual matters, but I could hardly tell him that I could see and speak to ghosts.

For some reason, my words seemed to upset Basil. He stood up abruptly. "That's what they all say," he said tersely, "but when crunch comes to crunch, it's another thing entirely." With that, he left the café abruptly.

CHAPTER 19

I awoke with a smile on my face. As I climbed out of bed and brushed the tangles from my hair, I couldn't help but be happy. Today we had a funeral booked. That meant a world of weight was lifted from my shoulders.

I was also happy because of my mother. The reason I was happy was because I took some delight in knowing that Mum was going to hate it. Just as she had hated our last celebrity funeral, which was KISS themed, this one was going to drive her even more nuts. The man who had died, a ninety year old named Melvin, had been an Elvis fan. I was excited to have an Elvis funeral, as that had been my spur of a moment idea back in Basil's office.

Melvin's wife had died some years ago, and his son, Aaron, was the one who had requested the Elvis funeral. Aaron Jennings was Melvin's youngest son, a spry sixty-nine year old with wiry grey hair and a pot belly. He had come into the office a few days before.

"I saw the article about that KISS funeral you did," the man had said to me as he fidgeted with heavy gold rings he wore on some of his fingers. His polo shirt was unbuttoned, showing off a tuft of chest hair which greatly resembled the hair on his head. He looked as though he had stepped out of a caricature skit on a comedy TV show and into real life.

"Oh, your father liked KISS?" I had asked.

"Not quite," the man said, shaking his head. "Elvis, the King. We both loved him. In fact, the whole family does. I know Dad would want something special."

And today was the day. The Elvis funeral was going to drive my mother crazy. She hated Elvis and always had. I had no idea why. I practically skipped down the steps and into the kitchen. My mother was there, sitting at the table.

"How could you do this to me?" she asked, from over a bowl of cereal.

I poured myself one. "I'm sorry, but we need the money. These celebrity funerals are bringing in the cash. We make more money from one of them than we do with three normal ones. I'm perfectly okay with you sitting this one out," I added, hopefully.

"No, of course not. You need me there," she snapped at me. "Don't be such a brat."

We ate in chilly silence, and I headed to the funeral home as soon as I could.

As soon as I walked in, Janet set upon me. "I think you need to see this," she said. She turned and headed for the corridor that led to the morgue and her work station.

"I'll set up some tables," Mum said, "and the decorations, although I'm the only one who seems to know that this is a funeral, not a party."

It was cold in the morgue, and I shivered, but Janet seemed right at home.

"I'm trying to do his hair," Janet said, leaning over the dead man. "He has experienced hair loss, but up to forty percent of women will lose a significant amount of hair in their lifetime. You could be bald by the time you're this guy's age."

"What great news," I said. "Thanks for sharing."

My sarcasm was lost on Janet, so she beamed at me. "You're welcome. Anyway, I can skip the Elvis hairdo, or staple his hair down."

"Will the staples show?"

"Maybe a little," Janet said with a shrug.

"Try it," I said.

Janet beamed again. I was pretty sure she was excited to use the staple gun on someone, so I hurried away as quickly as I could.

When I reached the front hall, I could hear Mum speaking to someone in the kitchen. I walked through the swinging doors and was both surprised and annoyed to see Ian there.

"Laurel, how great it is to see you, kiddo," Ian said.

"Ian, please don't call me 'kiddo,'" I said. "You can't be more than five years older than I am."

My mother clicked her tongue against the roof of her mouth, clearly unimpressed by my lack of manners. Ian was like a younger male version of my mother. The two of them together could probably make me jump off a bridge if I wasn't careful.

"Why are you here?" I asked the annoying man. "We aren't open."

"I asked him over," my mother said. "He brought the most delicious little tuna salad sandwiches over to a church potluck last week, and I wanted him to come help me make some for today."

"For what?"

"The wake, silly," Ian said.

"Mum, the family has ordered the food they want."

"Well, this can be a little extra," my mother said.

"Who is paying for it?" I asked.

"I am. It's just tuna fish."

I forced myself to swallow my anger. "Mum, there will be over fifty people here today. That's not just a couple of cans of tuna."

"I'll tell you my secret," Ian said, leaning over to me and speaking in an exaggerated whisper. "I don't drain the tuna."

With some difficulty, I resisted the urge to strangle Ian, and addressed Mum. "Mum, you will have to use your own money for this, not the funeral home's money."

My mother crossed her arms over her chest. "You think you can speak to me however you like. How hurtful is that? I'm your mother, and you choose to disrespect me this?"

Ian crossed his arms over his chest, too. "A child

should always heed their parent's advice. You should obey your mother. It is set down that a woman must obey her husband and her parents. If you followed a Godly life, you would know that already."

I took a deep breath, and then another. I did not trust myself to speak. Instead, I went out into the hall and opened a small closet there. I pulled out a vacuum and got to work.

By eleven thirty, we were ready to receive guests. Janet had brought in Melvin. He was lying in an all white casket. His hair was in full Elvis mode, and the only reason I could see the staples holding it there was because I knew they were there. As strange as Janet could be, she was certainly good at her job. Janet had already left, as she rarely hung around for anything other than what I paid her to do, and that suited me just fine.

I went to open the front door, and found Aaron, the deceased's son, walking up the steps to the porch.

"I'm a little early. Is that all right?" he asked. He actually looked pretty dapper in a black suit, although he still wore the gaudy rings on his fingers.

"Of course. This is your party so to speak, though 'party' probably isn't the best word," I said.

"Party is fine," Aaron said with a smile. "It's what Dad would have wanted."

I nodded and held the door open for him. "Did you bring that CD?" I asked.

He pulled the Elvis album from his jacket pocket and handed it to me.

"I'll be right back, but please help yourself to anything in the dining room." I motioned to the room to our right.

Aaron nodded and I walked away. Within a minute, Elvis was crooning over a gentle guitar through the speakers. The speakers could be heard in every room, including the restrooms. My mother was in the small kitchen, brewing some coffee with Ian. I imagined her scowling as she heard Elvis come on, and it made me smile.

Aaron was in the viewing room, standing over his father. "He named me after Elvis," he said. When I shot him a confused look, he laughed. "Elvis Aaron Presley."

I nodded. "Oh, I see."

"Elvis had a swagger to him, I suppose," Aaron said. "My father had the same swagger. In fact, he's missing something." He looked down at his deceased father. "He's missing a bit of his swagger."

Aaron reached into his pocket and pulled out a

pack of cigarettes. He took one from the pack and tried to set it between his father's lips. When he was unable to insert it, he simply rested on it top of his lips. Aaron didn't light it, of course, but I knew that when my mother saw it she was going to have a fit. I smiled again.

"He smoked the same brand that Elvis smoked. He was truly a fan," Aaron said.

Behind me, back towards the front hall, the doorbell rang. "Excuse me." I turned and headed for the hall, but my mother beat me to the door. I could tell because she screamed her next words.

"That's going too far!" she yelled.

I hurried forward to see who she was yelling at. I burst into the hall and my mouth fell open. My mother was standing by the open door, wagging her finger in the face of Elvis himself.

Of course, it was an impersonator, but the man looked uncannily like the King of Rock and Roll in his later years: high black hair, white jumpsuit, round belly, and large aviator sunglasses. I hurried forward, took my mother by the arm, and tried to pull her back. Ian stood nearby, his hand over his open mouth in a completely cheesy and fake pantomime of shock.

"Please, come in," I said to the man.

"Thank you. Thank you very much," Elvis said in a poor attempt at a Southern accent. He came through the door, and then another ten Elvis impersonators came through after him.

$\mathscr{I}$ couldn't believe my eyes. Eleven Elvis impersonators were standing in the front hall of the funeral home. Some were dressed as old Elvis, some as young Elvis, and others somewhere in between.

Aaron walked into the hall and clapped his beefy hands together. "All right!" he said with a grin.

"What is this?" my mother said, her voice high pitched and bordering on hysterical. "This can't happen!"

Aaron looked at her. "My dad was a member of the group. You're looking at the best Elvis impersonators in the state."

"They need to leave," Ian said, stepping forward. "This is a man's funeral."

"No, Ian, *you* need to leave," I said firmly, glaring at him. "This is what Melvin would have wanted."

"This is exactly what Melvin would have wanted," one Elvis said. He was wearing a black jumpsuit with a rhinestone dragon. Every time he moved even slightly, the rhinestones caught the light and gleamed and glittered.

"I've got to see him," another Elvis said, "and pay my respects."

The other Elvises all nodded in agreement. They all filed into the viewing room, followed by Aaron.

As soon as they were out of sight, my mother rounded on me. "You're making a mockery of your father's hard work," she snapped. Then she looked at Ian, who was nodding his head hard again and again. "Come on, Ian, they will not be eating our tuna!" They hurried into the dining room.

I walked through the dining room and into the kitchen. Mum and Ian were muttering to each other, and snatching up the silver platters they had loaded with tiny tuna sandwiches.

I had just finished brewing a large pot of coffee

when I heard the bell ring again. I knew I had better beat my mother to it—who knew who was coming in now? Once the viewing started the door would be propped open, but since it was still a little early, I hadn't done that yet.

Mum rushed to the door, and I wondered why she was so eager to open it, considering how appalled she was. If there was one thing she hated more than tacky themed funerals, it was Elvis. Then I remembered how much my mother loved to be offended, and I understood why she was hurrying. There was a good chance she was about to open the door and have something to complain about, and she wanted to make the most out of the opportunity.

I slipped around her and grabbed the doorknob, and then threw my mother a look that a normal person would have understood to mean to be quiet and not to yell at anyone, but with my mother, you never could be quite sure if she understood normal societal cues.

I opened the door, and I was pretty sure my mother was going to faint. There was Pastor Green, dressed up like Elvis.

"Good morning," he said, holding out a box of

donuts. "I know you always have such good food, but I thought I could help out."

"Thank you," I said, taking the box.

"You are a man of God!" my mother spluttered. "First KISS, now Elvis? What's next?"

The pastor smiled and shrugged his shoulders, his white sequined jumpsuit glittering in the light. "Who knows? Perhaps the next funeral will be Aerosmith. I quite like them."

My mother shook her head. Behind her, Ian came out of the dining room. If he was embarrassed by or for the pastor, he didn't show it. He went into full butt kissing mode. "Oh Pastor Green," he gushed, "how absolutely delightful and lovely to see you! I haven't seen you for a whole day, at least. Can I get you some coffee? Or a delicious tuna sandwich?"

"No thank you, Ian," the pastor said shortly. I think he grimaced, but I couldn't be certain.

Behind us, three Elvises came out of the viewing area, and were headed for the dining room. They stopped when they saw Pastor Green.

"Looking good!" one man said. He was an older Elvis.

"But this is Pastor Green!" Ian said, his voice filled with shock.

The pastor ignored him and addressed the Elvis. "Thank you, but I must say, your costumes are masterful."

"Hey, we don't wear costumes," another of the Elvises clarified. "We try to channel The King in everything we do."

The pastor nodded. "He would be proud."

"I have to say," the third Elvis said, "if my pastor was as cool as you, I would still go to church."

"Please, stop by mine sometime," the pastor said, and behind me I heard my mother sigh deeply. The thought of people who spent their free time dressing up like Elvis going to her church was probably too much for her to bear.

The three Elvises went on to the dining room, and the pastor went to mingle, just as other guests were arriving.

As appalled as most of the family and friends had been at the KISS funeral, this one was the exact opposite. Everyone loved it, and the Elvis impersonators weren't the only ones who had taken some fashion tips from the King of Rock and Roll. Pompadours, silky scarves, and the like were all on display.

I was in the kitchen brewing the fifth large pot of coffee when Ernie materialised.

"I have to say, these funerals are getting better and better," the dead man said.

No one was there with us, so I could talk to him without looking like a lunatic. "This is pretty cool, huh?"

"I'm a little disappointed to see you aren't dressed up," he said.

I shook my head. "Not in a million years, Ernie."

"So what's next? Music themed funerals are getting stale, don't you think?"

I laughed. "It's only our second one."

"I'm just trying to keep things fresh."

"Do you think a dead guy is the one who should be trying to teach me how to keep things fresh?" I teased him.

"That's not very nice," Ernie said with mock disappointment. He was an easy going guy, under the gruff exterior. "Anyway, I'm going to follow that girl around. Did you see her? The one with the red scarf."

"Ernie, she's half your age. And she's alive."

Ernie shrugged. "Can't win 'em all, right? She's a sight to be seen, though, that's for sure."

The ghost faded through the wall, and I smiled, shaking my head as I turned and finished with the coffee. I took the coffee to the dining room. My mother and Ian were sitting at the table, a plate of tuna sandwiches between them. The way my mother looked at anyone who neared her, I knew that if someone tried to grab one she would swat their hand away.

"Mum, what are you doing?" I asked.

"Someone has to eat these," she said.

"How many have you had?" I asked, raising a brow. She was looking a little green.

"Too many," Mum admitted. I looked at Ian. If my mother looked sick, he looked like he was going to be my next viewing.

"Ian, are you all right?" I asked.

He pressed his hand to his lips and shook his head, while waving his other hand at me.

"Don't talk to poor Ian. He's going to release," Mum said.

"Releasing isn't anything like knowing, is it?" I asked, unable to resist. "If he starts anything like that in here, I'll have to call the cops."

Ian struggled to his feet and hurried away in the direction of the restrooms.

"I don't know why you have to be so vulgar,"

my mother said, shaking her head. She took the tray of sandwiches and stormed off to the kitchen.

I sighed and went into the viewing room. It was less a viewing and more of a party.

Aaron came over to me. "This is great."

"I'm glad you think so."

"Dad is loving it, from up there," he said.

"I think so too." I didn't know what I thought about the afterlife, but I did know that Melvin wasn't hanging around as a ghost. I wasn't convinced anyone could see Earth from wherever they went. I thought that maybe the world of the dead and living were separated by more than just air.

"I have one request, though," Aaron said.

"What is it?' I asked.

"Can I light that cigarette Dad has? One last smoke before the end?"

I shook my head. I knew that after the staples had come at least a can and a half of hair spray. If there was flame anywhere near dearly departed Melvin, he would go up like dry tinder.

"I can't have smoking in here," I said. "I'm sorry."

Aaron shrugged. "It's all right. It's still a good time."

I smiled and nodded. In the corner Ernie was dancing to Hound Dog with the woman with the red scarf, but of course she didn't know. I had to do everything in my power not to roll my eyes. I left Aaron and headed back for the dining room, intending to gather up the discarded plates. I saw my mother and Ian heading out the front door.

"Where are you going?" I asked my mother.

"Ian and I are going to pray for these heathens," my mother said. "We're going to pray that they stop liking Elvis."

"What about Pastor Green?" I said. "He likes Elvis. Surely you aren't going to pray against your pastor's wishes?"

Ian's hand flew to his mouth and he gasped. My mother shot me a stony glare, and then grabbed Ian by the arm and pulled him down the stairs.

CHAPTER 21

*M*rs Anise showed me into Basil's office, after asking me my name three times in a row. The appointment was so that Basil could give me the projected figures for the coming year. Again, as soon as I was through the door, I smelt the strange smell that I now knew to be white sage. It felt old somehow. It reminded me of Grimms' Fairy Tales, or of storybook tales of witches.

Basil was sitting behind his desk, and he gestured to the seat in front of me. "Have a seat, Laurel." His voice was not unfriendly, but it was not warm.

Was I missing something? He had been happy and casual the other day at the café, apart from just before he left. I supposed this was his on-duty persona, although something told me there was more to it.

As he handed me a file, my arm brushed something on his desk. It was a silver framed photo of two sheep. I was so shocked that someone would frame a photo of sheep that I said without thinking, "Most people have family pictures on their desks." I kicked myself mentally. What a stupid thing to say! "I'm sorry, Basil," I said. "I shouldn't have commented."

Basil narrowed his eyes, and at once the room seemed to still. The feeling was almost tangible. "Unfortunately, I can't have a relationship," he said, picking up the photo frame and looking at it. "I don't intend to get married at this stage. Marriage and family are not in my plans." When he finished, he looked straight at me.

I squirmed in my seat. What on earth did he mean? Could he tell I was attracted to him and so had directed those pointed comments at me? My cheeks burned.

And why couldn't he have a relationship? All these thoughts and more swirled around in my head, and at the same time, I tried to push down my disappointment. Truth be told, I had thought there was a good chance that the hot accountant would ask me on a date sooner or later, but now my hopes were cruelly dashed. I tried to keep a neutral expression on my face, although I felt devastated. There was just something about the man that drew me to him.

Basil, thankfully, was not looking at me. He was looking fondly at the framed photo. "Do you have pets, Laurel?"

I shook my head. "I lived in an apartment in the centre of Melbourne, and pets weren't allowed. When I was growing up, I always begged my parents for a pet, but Mum wouldn't have any because they mess up the house." I tensed up as the memories flooded back to me. "I always wanted piano lessons, too, but Mum said a piano would ruin the décor. You know, I need to move out of Mum's house. I could renovate the apartment over the funeral home, but I couldn't have pets there." I caught myself, realising I had rabbited on at length, which I tend to do when I'm embarrassed. I bit a fingernail and looked at Basil.

"So what sort of pets would you like?" he asked.

"Dogs and cats," I gushed. "I would love a cat and a dog, but it's just not possible. Even if I did fix up that apartment above the funeral home and live in it, then I wouldn't be able to have pets due to health regulations."

"You could have a sheep," he said, his face lighting up. "Or rather, two sheep, because they need company."

I raised my eyebrows. Had he taken leave of his senses? Too much mathematics can't be good for anyone. "Sheep?" I said in disbelief. "Sheep as pets?"

Basil frowned. "Why not? It's only a construct of our society that people have cats and dogs as pets, and eat sheep. Sheep are just as clever as dogs and cats, despite what people tell you. They have individual personalities."

I thought it over for a moment. "That makes sense," I said slowly. "I've just never thought about it before." Basil was full of surprises. I never imagined that an accountant would keep citrine in his wallet or have sheep as pets.

Basil nodded. "You have that big paddock right next to the funeral home. Is that on your land or your mother's?"

I thought for a moment. "The paddock comes with the funeral home, so that was left to me in Dad's will. Mum owns the house on the small plot of land adjacent to it."

"And how do you keep the grass in that paddock down?"

"I have to pay someone to mow it, and he charges an arm and a leg, 'cause it's such a big area."

Basil rubbed his chin. "Is it five acres?"

I nodded, impressed. "Yes. How did you know?"

He shrugged. "Looks about right. And it's divided into two paddocks, isn't it?"

I nodded again. "Yes, but I don't know about having sheep as pets. I've never thought about it before. Aren't they hard to look after? And what about shearing, and all that?"

"It's easy enough to find shearers who'll come out to shear pet sheep," Basil said, "and as for looking after them, once you know what's required, it's easy enough. Besides, my two sheep are Dorpers. That means they don't need to be shorn, because their wool falls out."

"Fascinating," I lied. I had heard more about sheep than I had ever wanted to hear. "Why don't you put your sheep in my paddock? I won't have to pay for it to be mown, then." It was an off-hand remark, which I said without thinking. I really had to learn to think before I spoke.

Basil looked torn. In fact, he looked as if I had

put him in a terrible and earth-shattering dilemma. I just wanted to leave his office as fast as I could. Clearly he didn't want to be around me in anything other than an accountant-client capacity, but the thought of yummy grass for his sheep was too much to pass up. Why hadn't I kept my big mouth shut?

After what seemed an eternity, he finally spoke. "Thank you, Laurel," he said slowly, looking down at his desk while he shuffled papers around. "It's a good idea. I'll come over and check it out to see if it's safe. Once you get to know my sheep, perhaps you will want two sheep of your own. I'll pay you for boarding Arthur and Martha, of course."

I was doing my best not to burst out laughing at the sheep's names, so it was a while before I could trust myself to speak. "No, Basil, I won't hear of it. You'll be doing me a favour because I won't have to pay for it to be mown." *And I'll get to see you more often*, I added silently, but I didn't know whether that was a blessing or a curse.

As I left Basil's office, I turned on my phone. There were five missed calls from John Jones. I called him back, and he answered at once. "John, how did you get my number?"

"Your mother gave it to me. Laurel, I'd like to ask you out on a date."

"John, I don't mean to be rude," I snapped, "but this is an unlisted number. This is my private phone and I do not appreciate you calling me. I will not go on a date with you." I hung up.

By the time I got to my car, John Jones had called me three times. I hopped into the driver's seat and then blocked his number. I called my mother.

"What's the problem, Laurel?" she said. "John asked for your number. I couldn't lie, could I?"

I gritted my teeth. "Mum, we've been through this before. You can't give out my unlisted number to anyone."

"I can't lie, Laurel. You can't ask me to lie."

I groaned loudly. "Mum, I'm not asking you to lie. If someone asks for my number, just say this: 'It's an unlisted number and Laurel asked me not to give it out.'"

"Laurel, I don't know what your problem is, but I've already told you that I will not lie!" she yelled.

"But that's not a lie," I said, doing my very best to remain calm. "It's the truth."

"If you're not going to talk sense, I'll hang up." She did just that.

CHAPTER 22

I woke up early, as I always did on funeral days. I was at the funeral home two hours before the viewing started. Surprisingly, my mother had beaten me there. Also surprising was the fact that she wasn't alone. I pushed open the unlocked front door, and was at once face to face with an unsightly tangle of metal bars. Two men in white overalls were assembling the bars into something that might someday resemble scaffolding.

"Morning," one of the men said to me, putting a finger to the bill of his painter's cap.

I sighed and nodded to the man as I shut the door and walked past him and his friend. I consoled myself with the thought that at least they weren't Ian.

I found my mother in my office. The fact that it had never been her office didn't keep her from rushing in there and sitting behind the desk at every opportunity.

She was in a nice pantsuit and with her hair curled and piled upon her head. I supposed that meant she had not forgotten there was a wake today. A woman had died in her sleep a couple of days ago, and her husband had come to me in a horrible state. Some people knew exactly what they wanted for funerals, the type of flowers they wanted, the casket, and all of that. And some people, like the man with whom I had spoken two days ago, just wanted me to take care of everything. So I had.

"You're up early," I said as I leant on the doorway.

"We have work to do today," my mother said. She was staring at the computer. I had no idea why.

"I know. I was wondering if you had forgotten," I said.

"Of course I haven't forgotten. I haven't forgotten the schedule here in over thirty years, since your father opened the place. And thank goodness for today. Finally! A normal service, just a body and the people who loved that body, seeing it off."

I frowned. "That's a little morbid for you, Mum."

"I admit, working in this business does make death a bit mundane," my mother said. "As mundane as going to meet our Creator can be."

I came to the point. "Mum, there are painters out there."

"I know that, Laurel," she said in a frosty tone. "Do you think I'm stupid? Your father and you always thought I was stupid. How could you be so hurtful? Let me tell you, I'm not stupid, Laurel! Of course, I know there are painters out there."

I shook my head. "Mum, they're out there putting their metal pipes together."

"I told some men from the church that we needed new paint, and they said they'd do it for a bargain price." She looked so pleased with herself.

I sighed. "Mum!" I said, trying not to scream or have some sort of yelling episode. "We don't need new paint. I told you that when you brought it up a week ago. And even if we did, we certainly wouldn't have them do it before a service begins. The paint will still be wet."

Mum shrugged. "Laurel, you could appreciate me for once. Why don't you appreciate all the hard work I do for this business? You always were an ungrateful child."

I continued to take deep breaths. "You shouldn't have hired them. We don't have the money. I told you this before, and even if we did have the money, we couldn't have painters here while there's a service. Tell them to go, or I will, before they put a spot of paint on the walls."

My mother shook her head, and looked furious. "What an awful thing to say," she said, placing a hand over her chest. "I won't send Jerry and Bill away! You'll have to do it," she screeched.

"Fine," I said. I spun around and headed back to the entrance hall. The taller one had long swipes of eggshell white spread across the original wall, which had just been good old white.

"Oh no," I wailed.

He turned to me. "You don't like it? Your mother said you picked it out."

"No, it's fine," I said grumpily. They had already started. I couldn't have them stop now. "Can you please hurry?"

A look of disapproval passed across his face. "You can't rush good work." He waved his brush at me with a flourish. Globs of eggshell white flew from the thick bristles and fell on my carpet. I buried my face in my hands.

"Whoops," he said. Behind him his partner was finishing with the scaffolding, as if the ceiling was twenty feet high instead of nine. I could basically touch it if I hopped and reached. "That'll come out, Bill," he said to his partner, "but we should have spread some plastic. It's out in the truck. I'll go get it."

I nodded. "Thanks," I said. I tried not to say it sarcastically, but there was a good chance that sarcasm would be as lost on the painters as it was on my mother.

The other painter was younger. He had a tan face, and was stick thin. He sauntered over to me and looked me up and down. "I'm Bill," he said. "Your mother didn't tell me you were such a fox. I've never seen you at church."

"I worship the devil," I said angrily.

Bill's eyes widened and he stepped back. "Surely you're joking!" he said.

"Call me a fox again, and you'll find out," I snapped. I hurried into the kitchen before I said something I would regret and forced myself to focus on preparing the food for that morning. I had chosen turnovers and other pastries, as well as the usual coffee and fruit juices. The funeral service and the wake would be one after the other.

Some people had wakes over multiple days, to allow enough time for everyone who wanted to say goodbye to the deceased to do so, and some people, like the man I had dealt with for the funeral, wanted it all done as quickly as possible.

I thought of him as I set out pastries onto platters, and then covered them. It would be a while until the guests arrived, but the pastries had been in the refrigerator, so pulling them out early was a good idea. I took out one platter and set it on the dining room table, and then went to get another platter ready. It only took me about five minutes to set up a platter, but when I pushed through the swinging door and back into the dining room, Jerry was standing at the table, stuffing half a cherry turnover into his mouth.

"What are you doing?" I rushed over and set the platter down.

"Obviously, I'm taking a break," Jerry said, his eyes wide.

"A break?" I asked, and I went to the doorway and peered into the entrance hall. He hadn't got much further with his eggshell white than he had been when I had seen it ten minutes ago. "A break from what?"

"It took us a while to get that scaffolding up," Jerry said defensively. "Are you going to set out some coffee for us?"

"I'm not setting anything out for you." I shook my head. "This is for the service we have going on this morning. You can't eat anything else. I didn't even want you here today."

"I didn't know you had a service today," Jerry said. "You shouldn't have had us come today in that case. That just doesn't make any sense. Your mother said you weren't good at running this business." He shook his head in a solemn manner.

"I know you shouldn't have been here today," I said icily. "Please get out there and try to finish as fast as you can."

Jerry shook his head. "Thelma hired us for the whole place. It will take a day or two to paint that one room."

I squeezed my hands tightly, and felt the turnover oozing out between my fingers. "Please just go and paint," I said between clenched teeth. Mercifully, Jerry must have been able to tell that I meant business, so he did.

I was cleaning up the turnover when I heard

someone call my name from the doorway. "What?" I snapped as I stood and turned. Janet was standing there.

"I'm going to go down and finish her up," she said. "Are you okay?"

I nodded.

"There are men out here painting."

I nodded again.

"All right," Janet said, and then she left.

By the time Stuart, the deceased's widowed husband, arrived, half the entrance hall was painted. He navigated the scaffolding, and I hurried to shake his hand. "I'm so sorry about this," I said. "It was an emergency."

"Emergency painting?" he asked.

"I'll refund you ten percent of your bill," I said. "I can take it right off today and give you a new one."

"Oh no, it's fine," Stuart said. His eyes were red and raw. I figured he'd been crying all morning. "Can I see her?"

"She hasn't been brought up quite yet."

"Oh," he said.

"Please have coffee while you wait." I led the mourning man into the dining room. I poured him a cup, and he took it with a gracious nod of his head. A small bell chimed through our speakers, indicating Janet had the casket in place. "You can see her now," I said.

When we reached the viewing room, I opened the door for Stuart to go in, and I headed back to the front door. Just as I reached it, two elderly women came in.

"Is this the right place?" one of the women asked, nodding to the two men painting. They were both on the scaffolding, and I was worried it wouldn't take their weight. The scaffolding did not look sturdy at all.

"It is," I assured the woman. "Let me take you to the viewing room."

The two women nodded and followed me as we dodged around the scaffolding. Bill was painting right above the doorway, leaning out over the edge of the scaffolding. I was relieved that he at least knew not to set the scaffolding right in front of the doorway. As we passed through the doorway, I looked up to see that his brush was overloaded with paint.

I was about to say something, but it was too late. A large drop fell from the end of his brush, and landed right on top of the elderly lady's head. I didn't know whether to say something, but she didn't seem to notice, so I thought it prudent to remain silent. Today certainly couldn't get any worse.

When I returned to the entrance hall, my mother was there. She made an exaggerated show of sitting on a nearby chair and acting tired.

"Where have you been?" I asked her.

"On the phone in my office," she said. "I've been talking to people at church and trying to find someone to put in new carpet."

"Mum, no. Absolutely not." I was irritated at her use of the word 'my' to describe *my* office.

"This carpet is old."

I shook my head and did my best to speak in a calm tone. "Dad put in new carpet less than three years ago. We don't have the money for new carpet."

My mother shrugged and waved her hand at me as her ringtone, the screeched words, 'The wages of sin is death,' sounded. "I can't talk to you, now, Laurel. It's Ian on the phone." She disappeared from the office, telling Ian in a loud whisper that I was an ungrateful brat.

CHAPTER 23

"Hello?" I said sleepily into my mobile phone moments after I was startled awake the following morning.

"Hey there, is this Laurel?" asked a gruff voice I recognised right away. It was Stanley King, the man who ran the local mechanic shop. He'd had my car for almost a week.

I was quite fond of my little car. It was small and good on gas. It had always been dependable, at least until the other week.

"Yes, it's Laurel," I groaned. "It's early, isn't it?"

"We start at seven," the cheerful voice said. "Your car is ready to pick up."

"All right, thanks," I said.

Stan's shop wasn't more than five blocks from

the funeral home. When I got to the shop, the large garage door was pulled up, and my little car was there, ready to go. Stan came out, wiping his filthy hands on a rag that had probably once been red, but was so old it had faded to a soft pink. He wore overalls and a black cap pulled low over his brow. He was the only mechanic in town.

"Hey," Stan said as I stopped in front of him. "I wanted to give you some advice before I hand you these keys." He pulled the keys from the front pocket of his overalls. He held them out but didn't drop them into my palm.

"Okay, let's hear it," I said.

"You need to get rid of this car. You really should trade it in while you can. I fixed what I could, but it's all about to go."

"You're kidding!" I said with horror.

Stan shook his head. "With a car of this age and mileage, once something starts to go, other things will start to go. You'll have to start spending a fortune on it soon. It will need new brake pads, and shocks, and a whole lot more." He waved a print out under my nose and then dropped the keys into my hand. "It's all listed on here. Drive out to Tamworth. You should get a new car."

I sighed. "Oh dear." I thanked Stan and swiped

my card, and then I climbed behind the wheel of my car and sat for a moment. I needed to psych myself up to go to Tamworth and buy a car. I was never good in situations like that. I never knew whether or not people were ripping me off, and I never knew the right thing to say. I also didn't know where the money would come from. I did the only thing I could do in such a situation—I headed straight for the nearest café to load up on caffeine.

I was drowning myself in a half-strength latté, half strength as I intended to have several, when I heard someone clearing his throat behind me.

"Hey," I said, startled to see Basil there.

"You seem deep in thought," he said.

I nodded, at a loss as to what to say. I wondered if things were going to be weird between us after our last meeting, but he seemed fine, so I tried to push such thoughts away and do my best to appear nonchalant. Basil was peering at me, no doubt waiting for an answer, so I decided to tell him what had happened. "I've just come from the mechanic's shop. He says I need to go to Tamworth and trade in my car, 'cause it's starting to fall apart. I've had it regularly serviced, but that hasn't really helped. The mechanic said that the brake pads are going, then it's the shocks, the tires, you name it." *Shut up, you idiot,* I silently scolded myself. *Can't you say anything between nothing and your life history?*

Basil appeared nonplussed by my verbal outpourings. "Are you worried about the money?"

I nodded.

"You can charge the car to the business," he said.

"Really?" That was a new one on me, but then again, I was new to a running a business.

Basil took the seat across from me. "If you buy the car through the business, the interest on payments will become a tax deduction."

My face lit up at the words 'tax deduction'. "Really?" I said again. I shook my head. I had to learn how to speak like a normal person in the presence of such an attractive man.

Basil took a sip from his take-out cup. "When were you intending to do this?"

"Now," I said. "I was just getting a caffeine hit first, to boost my courage. I really don't want to go and buy a car. That sort of stuff freaks me out big time."

Basil smiled, and my heart fluttered. "I can go with you," he said. "I'm going to Tamworth today to meet with clients. I can meet you there in two hours." He produced a card from his wallet and slapped it on the table in front of me. "This dealership is good, and it's right on the highway. I'll bring your financial records. With me there, the financials for the business loan will all go smoothly."

"Wow, thanks so much, Basil," I gushed.

"Not a problem." He flashed a smile at me and stood.

I watched him go. I couldn't decide if I was more-or-less nervous now that he would be there.

The dealership in Tamworth was massive, a rolling paved lot with a thousand or so cars on it, or at least that's how it seemed to me. I parked just inside the lot, and looked around for Basil. There were two men in suits outside the main office door. They were talking to each other and appeared to be salespeople, but neither of them paid me any attention. I walked around the cars and looked in the windows, waiting for one of the men in suits to come my way, but they continued to ignore me.

Eventually, I saw Basil get out of his car on the street. No sooner had he reached me, than one of the men in suits was by our side.

"Hey there," the man said, offering his hand to Basil, who shook it. The man did not offer me his hand. In fact, he did not even look at me.

"Hi," Basil said.

"What are you in the market for?" he asked.

"Well, Laurel here is the one actually looking for a car," Basil said. "I'm just going to help."

The man nodded, as if Basil had said something interesting. "Great, so what were you thinking?" he asked. I thought he would be asking me, but he was still staring at Basil.

"I don't know. Laurel is the one who is looking," Basil said more forcefully.

Finally the man looked at me. He didn't offer me his hand, but just waited for me to speak.

"That's my car there," I said, indicating where my car was parked. "I like it, so something similar, I guess."

The man nodded, and then he turned to Basil. "Is she planning on trading it in?"

"Why don't you ask her?" Basil said shortly. I was pretty sure he was just about as annoyed with this guy as I was.

"Yes, I am going to trade it in," I said loudly and clearly.

The man turned and waved his hand to a man walking past.

"Check this car out, will you, Ben? What can we give these guys for it?"

The man turned to Basil once more. "Let's see

what we can find similar."

We walked around and around, with the man doing a heavy duty sales pitch. He addressed his sales pitch the whole time to Basil. After ten minutes or so, I found a car I really liked. It had only been used for test drives, and had a big sign on it: 'Huge reduction. Manager's special'.

We went inside and waited for the man to speak to his colleague. He came back and told me how much they would offer me for my car. It was more than I had been expecting, so I nodded my head and tried not to look too eager.

"As for financing," the man said, once more turning to Basil, "we can make you a good deal through our credit union partnership."

"It is Ms Laurel Bay who is buying the car," Basil snapped. "I am simply her accountant. I suggest you show Ms Bay to your financing department right now, or she will look at another dealership."

The salesperson did not appear to be offended, but kept smiling.

The man who handled the finances was uptight and officious, but all the paperwork went smoothly, thanks to Basil's help.

I drove home carefully, excited to have a nice

new car, but my enthusiasm was somewhat dampened by Basil. I could not help thinking of our last encounter. Today, Basil had been nice and helpful, but he had also been somewhat closed. He had made it clear that our relationship was to stay on a strictly professional level, but I wanted more, as much as I was reluctant to admit that to myself.

As I parked my new car in the driveway, Ernie came floating out through the front wall of the house. He whistled. "What a beaut," he said.

"Are you teasing me?" I asked. I could never tell with Ernie.

"Yes, that thing is ugly and plain as sin," he said.

"Don't let my mother hear that," I said, knowing full well she could never hear what a ghost said. "She'll be the first to tell you that sin isn't plain, although I guess she would agree that sin is ugly."

"You should have had me go with you if you were buying a new car," Ernie said. "I know my way around a car."

"Ernie, I thought you died before cars were invented."

"Very funny," the old ghost said with a grumpy frown. "I don't know why I'm your friend."

CHAPTER 24

*A*s I stepped into Hairway to Heaven, the only place in town to get a hair cut, I caught a glimpse of the stylist and thought about turning and running. Her hair was, to put it simply, a bit much. Piled high upon her head, and with blue and pink streaks running through it, it looked like something you would see on a fashion runway in Milan, where all the fancy fashion people worked so hard to make their models look as outlandish as possible.

The stylist had dark eye makeup and false eyelashes. There was nothing subtle about her. She was working on an older woman with greying curls who appeared to be asleep. The stylist glanced over at me and smiled. "You must be Laurel."

Too late. I had lost my chance to escape. I couldn't just turn and leave now. "Yes," I said.

"I'll be right with you. Have a seat."

I sat down on an uncomfortable seat and reached for some reading matter on the table in front of me. There were no magazines, only several King James Version Bibles all in black leather, three books, and a pamphlet with the intriguing title, *Turn or Burn*. I looked over the three books: *Fire and Brimstone* by Thomas Vincent, *Hell's Terror* by Christopher Love, and *A Few Sighs from Hell* by John Bunyan. I shuddered. Whatever happened to entertainment magazines?

I thought the pamphlet looked the most interesting as I thought it contained stories about fire-fighters, but it was a long diatribe stating that people who didn't repent were headed straight for hell. I gave up and stared blankly at the wall until the old woman woke from her slumber, her haircut apparently done. She paid at the small counter near the door, and then the stylist beckoned me over.

She smiled at me and pointed to her chair. There were three chairs, but no other stylists seemed to be working, or if they were, they were through a closed door that I imagined led to a back room, maybe a break room.

"Laurel, your mother told me at church last Sunday that you had to get in here, and I agree. You're letting that hair get way too long."

My hair wasn't any longer than it normally was, and I shrugged my shoulders. "I only want an inch or two off," I said.

"I'm Katy by the way, and there's no way an inch will do. I was thinking a lot more. It's one thing when I'm working on Elspeth—that's who just left —and I know, this might not be the best thing to say, but old women are simply set in their ways. They won't ·let me do anything fun, anything stylish!"

"I don't want anything fun or stylish, either," I said, when she paused for breath. I didn't think Katy's idea of fun was going to end up anything like mine. "I'm sorry to disappoint you, but I just want the split ends cut off."

Katy swivelled my chair, and I was staring into a mirror. She waved her hand at my reflection. "Don't be a party pooper," she said.

"My hair isn't a party, believe me," I countered.

"Let me just tell you what I was thinking. Can I at least do that? Let me tell you that, and then, if I can't convince you, we'll give you the Elspeth," Katy said with a chuckle. As frightening as it was to

225

be in a chair in front of this crazed woman with blue and pink in her hair, seconds from her doing something to my hair, I decided right away that I liked her.

"Okay, that's fair," I said. "Tell me."

Katy took a deep breath, and then launched into her pitch, her hands moving this way and that so I could see them in the mirror as she explained what she saw for the future of my head.

"Cut it short. I mean short. All right, and I know, you have this long hair, and it's beautiful, it really is, but short is in. I'm telling you right now, it's in. Short. Short, short, short. Shorter than Tom Cruise, all right? Like, to here. Can you see my hand? There. Okay, and then this gets shaved down, and a lot of women scream when they hear I want to shave their heads, but I'm telling you, this is movie star stuff. So we do that, and then I'm thinking hot pink. Streaks. I'm not crazy—it would just be streaks."

"Katy," I said, my eyes wide, "um, err." I was truly speechless.

She smiled at me in the mirror. "I knew it. I got you! I convinced you. Finally, someone in this little town who will let me transform them into a star."

"No," I said, and I felt a little bit bad as I

watched the woman's face fall. "I'm sorry, but no. Please just cut off an inch."

"All right," Katy said with obvious disappointment, holding up her hands. "You're the boss, right?"

I smiled. "Thank you."

The woman got to work. "Your mother tells me you took over your father's business."

I nodded.

"Sit still, girl, or you'll end up with a shaved head after all."

I laughed. "Sorry."

"Your father never came in here. I think your mother did his hair herself."

"Yes, she cut it for him," I said.

Mum had been cutting Dad's hair for as long as I could remember. When I was younger, I used to sit in the kitchen on the floor watching her. She cut his hair while he sat on a dining room chair that had been pulled over to the sink. That way Mum could easily sweep the linoleum tiles in the kitchen. She was never great at it, but my dad always let her do it.

"I thought so. Well, my uncle died a few years ago, and your dad was so great to my aunt and all of us. You know I go to church with your mother. I can't believe I haven't seen you there yet," Katy said.

"Church isn't really my thing."

I don't think that was what Katy wanted to hear from me, but to my enormous relief, she changed the subject. "You know, I cut the hair of only one regular guy, Lester Denning. Do you know him?"

"No, I don't think so," I said.

"He works over at the grocery store. He's the manager there. He's a really nice man, but strange too."

I could tell she was itching to drop some juicy gossip onto my lap, so I took the bait. "How so?" I asked. Her last client had been sleeping while she had her hair done, so the poor woman was probably itching to impart some good gossip.

"He wears make up. I swear it. I don't know if he dresses like a woman too, but he's come in before, and he has splotches on him that he's missed. It's mainly concealer and stuff. There's usually some under his ear, things like that. And you know, he keeps his hair so short, that I think he does it to put a wig on."

"It sounds like you find out some secrets," I said.

"Oh, that's nothing," Katy said happily. She was so interested in talking with someone new, I didn't even think she was upset about not getting to dye my hair pink and blue. "Do you know Martin Kaplan?"

I tried not to gasp. Martin Kaplan was my number one suspect in Tiffany's murder. "Sort of," I said carefully.

"Well, his wife, Louise, comes here. Did you know he was having an affair?"

"He was?" I asked, trying to sound shocked.

"Yeah, with that poor girl who died. You know, the one who was murdered."

I nodded. "I did her funeral."

"Right, well, that poor girl, sweet as can be, Tiffany was her name, she went to my church too, but she fell in with the wrong sort of man. Sleeping with a married man, it just isn't right."

"No, it isn't," I said when she paused for breath.

"Still though, that's something you work out with God, and I hope she got the chance when she passed. It's not for me to speak ill of her."

"So Martin Kaplan's wife knew he was cheating on her?"

"Yes, of course she knew."

"Was she very upset?"

The stylish shrugged. "She didn't seem that

upset about the cheating, 'cause she seemed more worried about the business."

"The café?"

Katy nodded.

"Why would she be worried about that?"

"Her grandfather had opened that café, and when he retired, her father ran it. Then, when her father was set to retire, he passed it on to Louise."

I wasn't quite following her train of thought, and hoped she'd come to the point soon.

"Well, with divorce laws and all that, since they'd been married for so long, he'd get half of the café, which means they'd have to sell it and split up the proceeds," she continued.

"I see," I said, hoping that I did. "So are you saying that if they got divorced, she'd have to sell the café that had been in her family for decades?"

Katy clicked the scissors at me by way of affirmation. "Exactly!" she said triumphantly. "That's right. She was really upset about that the last time she came in."

"When was the last time she came in?"

"Actually, it was the same day that Tiffany was killed," Katy said. "Louise had only just found out about the affair the night before. Boy, was she furious!"

I gasped. "So Louise Kaplan had the motive for murder!" My timing couldn't have been worse. Katy's scissors stopped and she turned to the counter. Standing there was Louise Kaplan.

"Is that new shampoo for coloured hair in yet?" Louise Kaplan asked Katy, while shooting a nasty stare at me. If looks could kill! Clearly she had overheard what I'd said.

Katy appeared unperturbed and rustled around in a cupboard, finally producing a giant bottle of shampoo along with a giant bottle of conditioner. Louise Kaplan paid for them and left abruptly, all the while glaring at me.

My heart was thundering so loudly in my chest I could practically hear it. Katy droned on, this time telling me about a client who'd had a child out of wedlock, but I wasn't listening. I nodded at intervals. By the time I paid, I had no idea what Katy had said, past the stuff about Tiffany and Louise.

I walked out of Katy's shop on legs that felt like they were jelly, and the drive home was a blur.

CHAPTER 25

J walked straight into the funeral home and called out for Tiffany. I knew it was safe to do so, as Mum was away at one of her many church meetings. This time, she had organised a prayer meeting to pray against Devil's Food Cake.

Tiffany materialised in front of me, making me jump and gasp. As familiar with ghosts as I was, I would never get used to their sudden appearances.

"What is it?" she asked. "I would say you looked like you've seen a ghost, but you know…"

Any other time I would have appreciated the joke, but now I couldn't even crack a smile. "I think Louise might be your murderer," I said.

"Louise? Martin's wife?" Tiffany asked.

"Yes."

Tiffany floated around to the other side of me. "Whatever would make you think that?"

"Could you perhaps, well, walk?" I asked. "If it isn't too much trouble. This floating thing kinda freaks me out."

"Not a problem," she said, as she lowered her feet to the ground. "Go on, tell me why you think it's her."

I took a deep breath and launched into my story. "Well, I was just at Katy, the hair stylist's, and she told me that Louise found out that Martin and you were having an affair just before you were murdered."

Tiffany shrugged. "It could be a coincidence."

I waved my finger at her. "Circumstantial evidence perhaps, but I've put it all together now. Louise is the murderer for sure! I'm going to call the cops."

"Behind you!" Tiffany said urgently, just before she vanished.

"Who are you talking to?"

I swung around to see Louise Kaplan, the last person I wanted to see. She closed the glass doors behind her and took a step towards me. Her face was contorted and menacing, her eyes narrowed and glittery. "You shouldn't spread rumours in a small country town. Who were you talking to?" She carefully put her bag on the ground. With one hand, she grabbed my wrist with her bony fingers and with the other, snatched my phone and looked at it. "Who were you talking to?" she asked again. "There are no recent calls on your phone."

I took a step backwards. "I was just thinking out aloud."

She released me and picked up the bag. "So you knew my husband was having an affair?"

This time I couldn't keep my mouth from hanging open. "Yes," I managed to say. "And the police already know, too."

"So? They haven't arrested me, have they! I was the victim in all this. I'm angry, and my anger hasn't gone away just because the little tart he was sleeping with is dead," she said. "I'm sorry if that offends you, but I didn't much like the girl."

"I understand," I said in a conciliatory tone. I had to think of a way out of this, and fast. She wasn't holding a gun, but she could have any manner of weapons in the big bag she was clutching to her chest. She was blocking my exit, otherwise I would just make a mad dash for it.

Louise jutted out her chin. "I heard you say you

figured out I was the murderer. You were about to call the cops."

"They won't listen to me," I said, looking around for something to use as a weapon. There was a huge potted plant, but there was no way I could lift it. There were two paintings on the wall, but I'd have to go past Louise to get them. I was backed up into a corner with no possible way of escape.

"I can't take that chance," she said. She reached into her bag and pulled out a large knife. I watched with strange fascination as the long blade reflected the fluorescent lights overhead. It all seemed surreal.

I've seen movies where intended victims manage to talk their way out of situations, but I couldn't think of a single thing to say. I was doing my best to focus on a way out when I heard a sound in the other room. "Did you hear that?" I asked her. "Someone's out there."

"Oh my God!" she said. "Do you think I'm stupid enough to fall for that?" She snarled and made for me with the knife.

Right then, my mother burst through the glass doors and hit Louise over the head with what looked to me to be a large, leather-bound Bible.

"Don't you take the Lord's name in vain!" my mother said to Louise, who had fallen to the floor in a heap and appeared to be unconscious.

Mum turned to me. "I've called the police. They'll be here any minute."

"But, what? How? When?" I stammered.

Mum appeared calm, if not rather offended. "You could at least thank me, Laurel. I heard what Mrs Kaplan was saying to you, so I called the police. I was waiting in the other room, but when she took the Lord's name in vain, I knew I had to act."

I tried to process that, but then thought it better if I didn't. "Thanks, Mum," I said dryly, "but I thought you were at church praying against Devil's Food Cake."

Mum shrugged. "I was the only one who showed, so I cancelled it."

"What does that tell you?" I said before I could catch myself. She had saved my life, after all, but I wasn't too happy about her motivation.

"That God works in mysterious ways," Mum said without missing a beat.

Duncan burst through the glass doors and stopped when he saw Louise lying on the floor, her large knife beside her.

"She intended to kill me," I said. "She admitted that she killed Tiffany."

Duncan pulled out his cuffs and bent over Louise, who was regaining consciousness.

Mum picked up her huge black leather-bound King James Bible and examined it for damage. "See, Laurel, if I'd used the Amplified Bible or one of those new little versions with the fancy paperback covers, who knows what would have become of you? Let that be a lesson."

"You lead the craziest life," I heard a voice say. I turned to see Tiffany standing next to the wall.

"Tell me about it," I said.

Mum looked at me. "Who are you talking to?" she asked, but fortunately Duncan's fellow police officer, Bryan, charged into the room at that point.

"Don't worry, Bryan," Duncan said as he stood up. "I took care of everything."

"Like hell you did!" my mother said. She slapped her hand over her mouth.

CHAPTER 26

For a moment my chest caught as panic seized me. I closed my eyes and forced myself to calm down. I remembered now. Last night, I had almost been killed. My mother, along with her King James Bible, had saved me.

My mother. I thought of her immediately. I jumped out of the bed and ran for the door. After a quick detour to the bathroom, I made my way into the kitchen. The clock on the stove told me in bold green numbers that it wasn't yet ten.

Ernie was leaning against the countertop.

"Coffee," I said, pouring myself a large mug. "I must get coffee, and fast. I slept in. My mother."

"I heard your boyfriend wants to put his pet sheep here," Ernie said with a snicker.

"He's not my boyfriend, Ernie," I said crossly. "He's just the accountant."

Ernie shrugged. "Whatever. But then you'll be able to do a ewelogy."

I nearly coughed up my mouthful of coffee. "That's not even funny," I scolded him. "Your puns are getting worse."

"I can tell you're cross by the look on your face," he said. "It's a dead giveaway."

I shook my head, left my coffee, and sprinted for the funeral home. I hesitated for a moment, thinking there was a possibility that Mum was at church. After what had happened, I wouldn't be surprised if she lived there for a month. Yet when I reached the funeral home, the front door was open. I knew that I had made the right decision.

I sprinted for my office. I might be safe—it was five to ten. To my dismay, there were voices inside. With my heart in my mouth, I pushed the door open.

Just as I had expected, my mother sat in my chair behind my desk. Across from her were two people. One was a woman, crying into a tissue. The other was Ian.

"Oh, this is my daughter, Laurel. She helps me here," my mother said dismissively.

I was amazed at how quickly the gratitude I had felt towards my mother the previous day had been replaced with a desire for her to move across the country forever. "Mum, can I speak with you?"

"One second," she said shrilly, holding up a finger at me. "We were just finishing up. Mrs Benson has lost her mother. We were looking into some packages."

I nodded and stepped outside, allowing my mother to finish. I thought it best, to avoid a scene in front of a customer. After Mrs Benson had been escorted out the door and was safely out of earshot, I glared at Mum. "What were you doing?"

Her eyes narrowed. "Someone needed to be here for the meeting. Did you forget about it?"

"No," I said. "Of course not. Mrs Benson was early. I arrived here with minutes to spare, to find you in my office conducting the meeting."

Mum stood up, and so did Ian. "You slept in," she said in an accusing tone.

"So what if I did?" I said. "I was still here in time. Anyway, I was almost killed yesterday. That was a frightening experience."

"Fear is not of God," Ian said, butting in. "I'm sure you feel closer to God now, dear."

"Why are you here?" I turned on him so quickly he flinched and stepped backwards.

"Perhaps I should be going," he said.

"Perhaps you should." I tried to glare a hole into the back of his head as he left.

"Laurel, I have no idea why you're always so rude," my mother said. "Is this the gratitude I get for saving your life?"

I ignored that. I knew that fact was going to be thrown at me forever. "Why was Ian here?"

"He was helping me. It's always nice to have someone lending a hand."

I rolled my eyes. "Lending a hand for what? Helping you tell people how many types of wood we can make coffins out of?"

"Don't be so smart, Laurel. You know we don't make the coffins," my mother said in a scolding tone.

It was all I could do not to scream. "Mum, please don't meet with clients with Ian. In fact, I would prefer you not to do it all."

Mum frowned. "I'm going to go to church." She left in a huff.

I went to the office and sat in my chair. I didn't even notice that Ernie had come in until he spoke.

"How you holding up, kid?" he asked.

"Fine thanks, Ernie."

"Tiffany was looking for you," he said. "She wants to say goodbye."

"She's, um, going on?"

The ghost nodded.

"Good. Where is she?"

"Out at her headstone, she said. She wants to meet you there. She said she was going to wait a bit."

I jumped up, not wanting to miss her. "Thanks, Ernie," I said as I ran for my car. For someone who was caffeine deprived, I sure was doing a lot of running.

I jumped into my car and sped off towards the graveyard. Tiffany was there, standing in front of her headstone. She must have heard me coming, or felt me, because she spoke to me without turning. "The police went to my house this morning. They told Mum everything about Louise."

"It must be nice to know," I said. "To have closure."

Tiffany turned to me. "For my mother, or for me?"

I shrugged. "Both."

Tiffany nodded. "Yes, it is. I know I feel better. I

feel lighter, which is a strange thing to say considering I can float."

"Please don't float," I said. "I'm glad you feel better. I'm only sorry it took so long."

Tiffany smiled at me and shook her head. "Don't be silly. Thank you so much for helping. No one else would."

I smiled, too. A man walked past and looked in my direction, but for once I didn't receive a strange look for talking to thin air. A cemetery was the one place where it was socially acceptable for people to speak to the unseen. "Well, you didn't exactly have a lot of people to ask."

"True," Tiffany said. The sun was in my eyes, and it made her a little hard to see, even for me. She was shimmering.

"So where do you go now?" I asked.

"That's the question, isn't it?" Tiffany shrugged. "I don't belong here." She shook her head softly.

"I know," I said. "Are you scared?"

"No," Tiffany answered. "I'm not. I think I should be, but I'm not. I know it will be okay. I can't explain it, but it feels really good—over there. I'm going to go now."

I nodded, sad that she was going, but pleased at the same time. Tiffany took another look at her headstone, and then the air around her grew brighter. All at once she took a step forward and then vanished. I knew I wouldn't speak with her again, as long as I was in this world. The thought of that made me sad, but I was happy for her. She had found closure, and she wasn't tied to this world any longer.

I turned and walked slowly back to my car, and then I drove home. My mother was still at church, so I walked out and looked at the five acre paddock where Basil was probably going to put his two pet sheep. The grass was already getting long again, and it had only been mown a week ago.

I thought about the people I cared about. There were people who were still in my life, like Tara, my mother, and Basil. I had no idea whether Basil would ever be any more to me than an accountant, but at least I could rely on him. If nothing else, he could be a friend, although truth be told, I wanted more than that. And there were people who were no longer in my life, like Tiffany and my father. Just because I couldn't speak with them anymore, it didn't mean I didn't care about them, and it didn't mean they didn't care about me.

I stood at the fence, thinking about Tiffany and about everything that had happened in the last few weeks. I wondered if I would be able to go so willingly to the other side when it was my turn. Still, ghosts—the ones without unfinished business on earth, that is—wanted to go to the other side. When they caught a glimpse of it, whatever they saw there made them happy. I used to think the saying that we are souls having a human experience for a time was just an empty saying, but now I knew it was true. Life doesn't end when we leave our earthly bodies; it continues.

I smiled and walked along the fence line. I was back here in Witch Woods and I was happy.

I couldn't believe I thought that being back in my hometown, running my father's business, actually made me happy. It had been a big change, but it had turned out to be a welcome one. I was running a business, and so far, and no thanks to my mother, I hadn't run it into the ground. I helped people daily. I helped people move on.

I supposed moving on wasn't the right term. We never really moved on. You didn't lose someone you loved and then just go on with life. There was always a part of them that went with you, and there was always a part of you that left with them. But that was okay, because I knew that the people, good or bad, who help make your life what it is are the most important people you'll ever know. I thought of Tiffany. I would miss her. I was glad she had crossed over, and I knew I would never forget her.

I made my way to the funeral home. I turned back when I heard someone call my name. Basil was waving and smiling as he walked down the fence line towards me, a sheep on a leash on either side of him.

NEXT BOOK IN THIS SERIES

WITCH WOODS FUNERAL HOME BOOK 2

Nothing to Ghost About

Laurel Bay is conducting a funeral when someone is strangled in the bathroom. Now that there have been two deaths in the funeral home, business is as dead as a doornail. As Laurel sifts through the clues, she is faced with too many suspects, a wisecracking ghost, and a woman journalist who appears to be after more than Basil's files.

Laurel thought that inheriting the funeral home was an opportunity to die for, but it seems to be quite an undertaking.

ABOUT MORGANA BEST

USA Today bestselling author Morgana Best survived a childhood of deadly spiders and venomous snakes in the Australian outback. Morgana Best writes cozy mysteries and enjoys thinking of delightful new ways to murder her victims.

www.morganabest.com